The Freedom Trail Mystery

NANCY SPECK

FOUR COR   CO.

NEW YORK

Four Corners Publishing Company
45 West 10th Street, Suite 4J
New York, NY 10011

Printed in U.S.A.
Maps © 2001 Mapping Solutions, Anchorage, AK.
Cover illustration by Bill Farnsworth.
Design by Kris Waldherr Art and Words.

09 08 07 06   6 5 4 3

Cataloging-in-Publication Data

Speck, Nancy.
  The Freedom Trail mystery / Nancy Speck. — 1st ed.
  p. cm. — (Going to series)
  SUMMARY: While at a summer field hockey camp in
Boston, Maine natives Serena Marlowe and Carly Heiser
stumble upon an unusual thief who is stealing historical
artifacts from Boston's Revolutionary War days. Their
pointed guidebook and a map of Boston are included.
Audience: Ages 9-13.
ISBN 1-893577-07-4

  1. Field hockey—Juvenile fiction. 2. Boston (Mass.)
—Antiquities—Juvenile fiction. [1. Field hockey—
Fiction. 2. Boston (Mass.)—Antiquities—Fiction.] I.
Title. II. Series.

PZ7.S7412Fre 2001   [Fic]
                                QBI01-700015

*For Uncle Don for his Boston help
and for Brian, my strength*

CONTENTS

CHAPTER ONE

Packing for Adventure

 Serena rearranged her shorts, T-shirts, underwear, socks, Bun-Bun, and Mr. Monkey in her duffel bag and yanked on the zipper again. It moved a few more inches and stopped, stuck now on Bun-Bun's ear. Serena knew she should probably leave her stuffed animals behind, but they'd always gone everywhere with her, and she saw no reason to exclude them from going to field hockey camp. She pushed Bun-Bun down with one hand and inched the zipper over the rabbit's ears. Finally clear, the teeth locked together and the zipper glided to the end.

Serena yanked the bulging bag onto the floor and began packing yet another duffel bag, this time with her goalie equipment. She dumped her helmet, chest and leg protectors, padded shorts, neck guard, "moon boot" goalie shoes, gloves, and goalie stick into the bag. She didn't even attempt to pull the zipper over the lumpy mass. Serena was just glad it all fit into the bag, making her equipment easier to carry.

"I think that's everything," said Serena to Tux, "unless you want me to pack you in here, too."

Tux blinked at her and promptly began washing his leg.

"I'm leaving for two weeks, and all you can do is take a bath." She flopped down onto the bed next to him and scratched the white V of fur under his neck, which resembled a man's tuxedo shirt. Within seconds the roar of his purr filled the room.

"You better hurry," called her mom from downstairs. "Carly and her mom will be here any minute."

"Coming," Serena hollered back. After kissing Tux on the head, she rolled to her feet. She grabbed the duffel bags and fell onto the bed again. "Hey, Maddie. Come help me with my bags."

"No way," came a voice from the room next door.

"Maddie!"

No answer. Serena pounded the wall of the adjoining bedroom with her fist. Tux jumped and stared, wide-eyed, at the wall.

"Madelyn!"

"Maddie, go help," said Mom.

Eleven-year-old Maddie appeared in the doorway, a scowl on her face. "I wish you were going to Boston permanently instead of only two weeks."

"Just make sure you stay out of my room while I'm gone."

"Maybe I will, and maybe I won't," sang Maddie.

Serena grabbed a duffel bag and slung it at Maddie, nearly knocking her over. Maddie tugged the bag by the strap and dragged it down the steps. Serena followed with the goalie equipment bag.

"Wow, Mom!" exclaimed Serena when she reached the bottom

of the stairs. Facing her was a large, framed painting propped against the wall. "You finished your painting."

"I've been cranking them out, haven't I? Can't miss the peak tourist season."

"I'm glad I'm missing it this year," Serena said.

Although she loved Bar Harbor, where her family had lived for four years, Serena had grown to detest the summers, when the streets were clogged with tourists on their one-or-two-week vacations, filling every campsite, motel, and cottage for miles around. The worst part of the tourist season was the first two weeks of August. Everyone on the Eastern seaboard headed up Highway 1 to Mt. Desert Island off the coast of Maine. At least it seemed that way to Serena.

Acadia National Park was the destination point, and Bar Harbor, the closest town, was home base for the vacationers. They jammed the sidewalks as they traipsed from store to store buying moose T-shirts, blueberry jam, and lighthouse hot pads for friends and family.

But the tourists, Serena knew, provided jobs for both of her parents. Her mother owned Maine-ly Paintings, a gift shop filled mostly with her original paintings of Maine scenes. Her father piloted a tourist boat, the *Marta*, named after her mother, which he'd bought after retiring from the Navy. Twice each day in the summer, he sailed vacationing families into the open ocean in search of whales, dolphins, and puffins.

Serena and Maddie and their brother, Kyle, had made many

trips with him, crashing through the whitecaps on a rough sea or gliding smoothly over the surface on a calm day. The condition of the sea mattered little to the Marlowe kids; they didn't possess a seasick bone in their bodies, unlike their mother who became queasy even before the boat left the pier.

When Serena was younger, she had greatly enjoyed accompanying her dad on the *Marta* or helping her mom arrange paintings and other gifts in the shop. But this summer, Kyle had left for the United States Naval Academy in Maryland, and Maddie had insisted that, at eleven, she was old enough to help Mom in the shop.

That was fine with Serena. In fact, when Coach Montkin had announced the field hockey camp at Boston University, Serena had wanted to go so badly that she had purposely played up to Maddie, telling her that she was really grown up and could help Mom in the store. Maddie had fallen for her flattery and soon was begging to help out at Maine-ly Paintings, too. Mom had agreed after only minimal nagging from Maddie.

A few days later, Serena had overheard her parents talking, laughing actually, at Serena's setup of her little sister. But Serena didn't care if they were wise to her. She was just grateful to be leaving Bar Harbor and escaping the tourist turmoil that transformed her slow, comfortable town into one large traffic jam.

"Are you sure you've packed everything?" asked Serena's mom. "Your retainer, cold sore medication?"

Serena sighed. "Yes, Mom. I didn't forget a thing." Serena wished she wouldn't still treat her like a kid.

"What about your camera?"

"Oops." Serena hurried back up the steps to her room. A minute later she rejoined her mother and sister with her Polaroid slung over her shoulder.

"Okay, then. Maddie and I need to get set up at the shop. Your dad said to say good-bye since he had that early morning breakfast tour."

Serena nodded. "We said our good-byes last night."

"Just lock the door when Carly and Mrs. Ritchie get here." Her mom stopped then, and Serena saw the moistness in her mother's eyes and felt the same reaction in hers. Her mother wrapped her arm around Serena's shoulder. "First your brother leaves for the academy, and now you're leaving."

"It's only two weeks, Mom," said Serena, assuring herself as much as her mother that two weeks wasn't long at all.

"Well, have fun and be careful. Boston's a big city, and you're used to life in a small town, on an island no less."

"Sure, Mom. I'll be fine."

Her mom gave her one final hug and was out the door.

"See ya, Twerp," said Serena.

"See ya, Hockey Head," answered Maddie.

Serena waved to them as the car backed out of the driveway and then began searching for a van to pull in. She couldn't wait to see Carly. Carly had spent the last three weeks with her dad in Houston and had only returned the day before.

Carly Heiser was Serena's best friend. She lived just a few blocks away and had spent her whole life on Mt. Desert Island. When Serena had first moved to Bar Harbor, Carly had introduced her to the kids in town and at school, a big help since Serena was used to life on a naval base and had never socialized much with the kids from the nearby towns. Carly had also eased Serena's worries about fitting in. Although Serena's dark skin, black hair, and Filipina features contrasted sharply with Carly's milky white, freckled skin and strawberry blond hair—indicating her Irish roots— Carly's friendship with her put to rest any worries Serena had had about other kids finding her different.

During her first weeks in Bar Harbor, Carly had taken Serena to all her special places around the island and in Acadia National Park. She'd led her to the best tidal pools to find crabs, sea urchins, and starfish. They'd hiked secluded beaches to hunt for driftwood and colored rocks, sanded smooth by the pounding surf.

Carly had also shown Serena her "secret sand bar," as she'd called it when she was little, which connected Bar Harbor to Bar Island. They had spent hours watching the tide go out, ever so slowly exposing a sandbar in the inlet, enabling them to walk to Bar Island. Another time, when Serena had spent the night, Carly's mom had driven them down to the water's edge at three in the morning so they could see the tide roll back in, eventually covering the sandbar, hiding the harbor's secret again. That adventure and others like it had helped Serena fall in love with the island, all because of Carly.

The girls also shared an enthusiasm for field hockey. Both had tried out for and made the team in seventh grade. Carly played middy, which meant she ran constantly, helping move the ball up the field to the offensive forwards and assisting the sweeper and goalie in defending the goal cage.

A van pulled into the driveway and honked. Serena opened the door and wrestled her baggage onto the porch. Carly, seeing the battle with the bags, jumped out of the van to help.

"What on earth did you pack?" she asked, laughing at the overstuffed luggage.

"Same stuff you probably did," replied Serena.

They lugged the bags to the driveway, hoisted them into the back seats of the van and then crawled into the middle seat.

"Hi, Serena," said Carly's mom. "Missed seeing you the last few weeks."

"Same here," Serena replied. She turned to Carly. "I was totally bored without you. So how was Houston?"

"It was terrific. My dad took me to a rodeo, and I got to see Brianne. She's cute, but she cries a lot." Carly hesitated.

Serena knew Carly had stopped talking about her new half sister because her mom was right there. Even though her parents had been divorced for three years and both had remarried, she always felt awkward talking about her dad when her mom was present.

"Look what I got," Carly continued quickly. She reached under the seat and pulled out a white cowboy hat.

"Ride 'em, cowgirl!" yelped Serena. She slapped her leg like she was cracking a whip.

"Planning to wear that on the streets of Boston?"

Carly snickered. "Of course not."

"Why not? A cowboy hat would really turn some heads."

"I don't want people staring at me. You wear it."

"Maybe I will." Serena put the hat on. "Howdy, pardner," she said with a country-and-western twang in her voice. "Call me Tex. And don't get me confused with my cat, Tux."

"You're crazy," Carly giggled.

Both girls laughed again and settled into their seats for the six-hour drive to Boston.

"Wow, look at the traffic," said Carly.

"It's nuts!" exclaimed Serena.

"I'm glad we're headed the opposite direction," Mrs. Ritchie muttered.

As they drove over the bridge to the mainland, they stared at the bumper-to-bumper traffic lined up, Serena knew, for miles, barely moving. Serena took one more look at the island disappearing behind her and then turned to Carly.

"Good-bye, Bar Harbor. Hello, Boston," she sang out.

They smacked their hands together over their heads in a high five, jarring each other so hard the cowboy hat popped off Serena's head.

"Here's to two weeks of fun," said Serena in her country-and-western voice again.

"And field hockey."

"And adventure in . . ."

"Boston!" they both shouted.

CHAPTER TWO

Are We Almost There?

 Serena fiddled with the air conditioning vent next to her, directing the cool stream of air towards her legs. The morning sun had beaten in on her for the past hour, first on her face, then her stomach, and now her thighs. She shifted in her seat, but it did little good.

She and Carly had talked rapidly for miles, filling each other in on their three weeks apart. Carly had told her about the rodeo she'd seen with bronco riders, cattle ropers, and rodeo clowns. Serena recounted that a tourist on her dad's boat had punched Hal, one of the guides, when he'd gotten off the boat. The passenger had spent the entire four-hour trip throwing up in paper bags and needed to vent his anger on someone.

That story had prompted Carly to describe in vivid detail the storm her plane had flown through on the way home. The turbulence had been terrible, causing several people to use the airline's paper bags to throw up in. They'd laughed as they'd wondered if the same company made barf bags for both planes and boats. Their conversation had lagged then, as all conversations are eventually fated to do for lack of fresh topics.

Serena peered out her window, marveling at the number of souvenir and collectibles shops that had opened along Highway 1. The hottest items appeared to be lobster traps and especially their buoy markers. Each sported a different pattern of colors in bright shades of red, orange, yellow, even lime green for easy finding on the dark water. But what exactly people did with them when they arrived home, Serena didn't know. She decided they probably ended up hanging in a remote corner of a basement rec room, forgotten and dusty.

"Have you ever been to Boston, Serena?" asked Mrs. Ritchie, jarring Serena from her thoughts.

"No," she replied. "We've driven around it plenty of times on the way to somewhere else, which is what we did in June when we took Kyle to the naval academy. But I've never actually been in the city."

"You'll love it," Mrs. Ritchie said. "There's so much history in Boston. Carly, her dad, and I visited Boston a number of years ago when I was researching historical sites for an article. I think Carly was three."

"Fortunately, I don't remember what must have been a boring experience," said Carly.

Her mom sighed. "History is not boring, Carly."

"The shopping in Boston sounds a lot more exciting to me," Carly answered.

Mrs. Ritchie ignored Carly's comment and glanced back

at Serena. "By the way," she said, "are you doing a history project this year?"

Serena nodded. "Yep. I'm doing it on the whole story of the *Titanic* and its aftermath. Mr. Cantwell is helping me learn how to study artifacts recovered from the ship and other kinds of historical artifacts. They've found people's glasses, jewelry, shoes, bottles of wine, plates they ate from. It's all so amazing and it really helps tell the story."

"Why are you doing a history project?" asked Carly. "It was only required last year because Mr. Cantwell made us do one. And you weren't all that thrilled about doing it then as I recall."

"That was before I'd really started to listen to Mr. Cantwell. I always thought American history was just a bunch of facts and dates I helped my mom learn for her U.S. citizenship test a few years ago. I could never understand why she was so eager to learn all that stuff. She said that becoming a citizen was the most important thing ever to her because the United States has a great history, which encourages Americans to look to the future and to improve things for the people—or something like that.

"I never really understood what she was talking about until we had Mr. Cantwell. He helped me understand how our past shapes our future. When I looked at history that way, I realized how important it is. That's when I got really hooked on history, I guess."

"Yeah, sure, the sinking of the *Titanic* in the North Atlantic in 1912 helped shape our future in a really positive way," remarked Carly sarcastically. "How many people died?"

"Fifteen hundred," answered Serena. "And that's just the point of the project. Because it was such a big accident, passenger ships after that had to have enough life boats for all passengers; ice warnings had to be reported right away; and the radio had to be on all the time.

"And the whole idea of a sinking boat gives me the shivers anyway," continued Serena, her voice low. "I mean, my dad served on Navy boats for twenty years, through the Gulf War and everything. His boat could have been attacked and sunk. And now my brother will be on a ship in another few years. Who knows where he'll be assigned? Then there's the storm I survived with my dad on the *Marta*."

"Yeah," said Carly. "I remember. You were afraid to get on the boat for weeks."

"I know. Then my dad pointed out all the safety and rescue features there are, and I was okay again. That's why this project is so important to me. All the past sailing successes and failures have brought us to our current level of standards for fully equipped boats and safe sailing. I know that my dad and Kyle are as safe as possible on their boats. Plus, the future may bring even greater improvements to ships.

"And it's the artifacts that serve as the link to remembering all of the successes and failures of the past, the successes inspiring us in our present and future endeavors and the mistakes establishing a memory so they're never repeated."

"I couldn't have said it better myself," laughed Mrs. Ritchie.

"Well, to be truthful," said Serena, "that's a rough quote from a book I borrowed from Mr. Cantwell." She turned to Carly. "While you were gone, I called Mr. Cantwell to see if he had some books on the *Titanic* and its artifacts. When I picked them up, he showed me some of the neat old things he has. Practically his whole house is decorated with antique furniture, and he has old books and tools and lots of antique kitchen utensils. He showed me how you can determine the date of an antique based on the quality and condition of the metal or wood."

Serena took a breath and continued. "Anyway, when we visit Kyle in Annapolis over Thanksgiving, we're stopping in Washington, D.C., when the traveling Titanic Museum is there. I should be able to find a lot of interesting stuff to add to my project."

"Speaking of artifacts," said Mrs. Ritchie, "you'll find plenty in Boston that tell the story of colonial life and the Revolutionary War. You two should walk the Freedom Trail while you're there."

"The freedom what?" asked Carly.

"It's a trail through Boston that takes you to a lot of the historical places, isn't it, Mrs. Ritchie?" questioned Serena. She turned to Carly. "Mr. Cantwell told us about it in history. Don't you listen to anything in class?"

"About as much as you do in computer class," quipped Carly.

"Touché," said Serena as she pretended to stab herself with the point of a dueling sword. "You got me on that one."

The two girls had been good-naturedly poking each other since they'd read a story in literature class on medieval knights who dueled with long, skinny lances. Whenever one of them got the better of the other in some way, one, or sometimes both, acknowledged the win or defeat with a "touché."

"There's literally a trail marked on the sidewalks that leads you to each site like Paul Revere's house and the Old North Church," continued Mrs. Ritchie.

"I read in our camp information packet that we go to Paul Revere's house and the Boston Tea Party Ship during a field trip the first Saturday," said Serena. "So we'll get to go on part of the trail."

"Is there a shopping trail in Boston, too?" asked Carly.

Serena and Mrs. Ritchie laughed. "I hope not," said Carly's mom.

As they traveled on down the coast through each small tourist town, the traffic slowed again. Serena was anxious now to leave the tiny coastal villages and to begin experiencing the big city. Boston, she knew, had a population of about five hundred thousand people, huge compared to Bar Harbor, but not as enormous as Philadelphia with four million or New York with seven and a half. Half a million felt like a good number to her.

In her American history class the previous year, Mr. Cantwell had discussed the Revolutionary War and Boston's part in the birth of the nation. Serena remembered that in the 1700s, many

Bostonians were growing discontented with the high taxes that the British king had placed on imported goods. British soldiers were sent to Boston to enforce the taxes. The colonists, in their pursuit to improve their lives by living under their own rules and not those of some distant king, joined forces against the British, resulting in war and, finally, independence.

Serena knew these were the first Americans who stood up for their rights and fought to improve their future. Their success enabled future generations to fight for and defend the country, including her father and now her brother as part of the Navy. It seemed to Serena that her whole family had a special link to America's past as well as its present. And she couldn't wait to experience the city where this first unification of its people had occurred. She knew that visiting Boston's old buildings and viewing the artifacts of its history would bring this incredible period to life for her.

"Are you two getting hungry?" called Mrs. Ritchie from the front seat.

Serena and Carly eyed each other and nodded.

"Keep your eyes open for a place to eat then," she said. "We're almost into Freeport, so we can stop there."

But several miles out of the tourist town boasting dozens and dozens of outlet shops, the traffic snarled into a knot. Mrs. Ritchie decided they should grab some sandwiches and eat in the van to save time. As they neared a small café, Serena and Carly jumped out to buy the sandwiches. A few minutes later they caught up to Carly's mom, who'd traveled less than a block in the traffic.

"I'm glad you found me when you did," said Mrs. Ritchie. "Otherwise I'd have turned at the next corner and then really been stuck in this jam. I sure wish there was a way out of this mess."

While they ate their turkey subs, Carly studied a map she'd picked up inside the café. She navigated her mom up and down the alleys and side streets of Freeport, bypassing most of the traffic. A few miles later they picked up the Maine Turnpike. Serena hoped it would now be smooth sailing the rest of the way into Boston.

By four o'clock the sun had begun to angle in on Serena from the window on the other side of the van. She picked up Carly's cowboy hat and plopped it onto her head to shield her eyes.

"I wonder what Boston University's like?" she mused.

"I looked it up on the Internet," said Carly. "It's located right along the Charles River, so that should be pretty cool."

"I wonder what the other girls will be like and where they're from," Serena said.

"It won't be long until you find out," answered Mrs. Ritchie. "We should be close to Boston."

The girls began craning their necks for a glimpse out the front windshield. "I see some buildings!" exclaimed Serena.

"Me, too," said Carly a second later. "What's that super tall building?"

"That's the John Hancock Tower," her mom answered. "It's Boston's tallest building. I think it's even the tallest building in New England."

"Could you imagine a building that size in Bar Harbor?" asked Serena, laughing at the thought of it.

"A colleague of mine wrote a piece on the Hancock building," said Mrs. Ritchie, "back when it was built, sometime in the seventies, I think."

She went on to explain that there had been a problem with the window structure and many of the huge glass windows kept popping out on windy days and crashing to the street below. Making matters worse, engineers later discovered the building was in danger of toppling over.

Carly shuddered. "I'm not going anywhere near that building," she said firmly.

"Workers fixed all the problems, so it's fine now," her mom reassured her.

"I'll bet there's one terrific view from the top," said Serena.

"I don't intend to find out," Carly added.

"You have no sense of adventure."

"Not when my life's in danger."

"Touché!" they said together, each stabbing the other with her imaginary sword and laughing.

They drove along the Charles River enjoying the view of the Boston skyline of tall buildings dominated by the greenish-colored glass of the Hancock building rising above the others. Sailboats

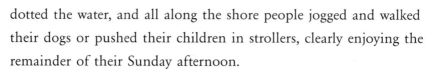

dotted the water, and all along the shore people jogged and walked their dogs or pushed their children in strollers, clearly enjoying the remainder of their Sunday afternoon.

"Carly, check the map," said her mom.

"Boston University is just ahead," answered Carly within seconds of locating their position. "Turn right at the next corner."

Mrs. Ritchie turned, and immediately campus dorms and other buildings came into view. Red and blue flags with BU printed on them hung from lampposts, announcing that they had officially entered the Boston University part of town.

"Look at the huge CITGO gasoline sign!" exclaimed Carly.

"That's certainly advertising in a big way," laughed Serena as she eyed the enormous sign rising from the top of a building.

They passed more dorms and other university buildings tucked among stores and restaurants of busy Commonwealth Avenue. Carly followed the directions in her camp information packet and told her mom to turn right at Babcock Street.

"There it is!" yelled Serena. "Sleeper Hall. We're here!"

CHAPTER THREE

Boston at Last

 Carly's mom pulled into the parking lot across the street. She had barely finished parking before the girls had flung open the sliding door and hopped out of the van. They raced to the other side of the street and up a set of steps to a courtyard bordered by three high-rise dorms and found that Sleeper was the one in the middle with Rich and Claflin on either side. Their attention, however, quickly turned to the enormous field and stadium located behind the dorms.

"What a field!" exclaimed Carly.

"Why is the grass such a funny shade of green?" asked Serena.

"Because it's not grass," answered Carly. "It's artificial turf or some kind of fake grass, like they have in professional football stadiums."

"You're joking."

"Nope."

Serena shook her head. Then suddenly she inhaled deeply. "Do you smell chlorine?"

Carly sniffed and walked towards the building next to

Rich Hall. "The pool must be in there."

Back at the van, the girls filled in Mrs. Ritchie on their discoveries while they unloaded their duffel bags. Carly spied her camera bag, unzipped it, and took out her camera.

"You aren't starting with the pictures already, are you?" groaned Serena.

"Sure, why not?"

"Because there's nothing to take a picture of yet."

"Are you kidding? How about the outside of the dorm and the playing field?" Carly aimed the camera at the dorm and pushed the button. She changed lenses then, and shot close-ups of the playing field.

"Well, I'm saving my film for sightseeing," said Serena.

The girls hauled their bags across the street and up to the front door of Sleeper Hall. "Wait there," said Carly. "I want to take a picture of you in front of the dorm."

Serena sighed but said nothing. She had posed for dozens of Carly's pictures and knew there was no use fighting what would be the usual long process.

Carly's mom was a photojournalist. She developed her own pictures in a darkroom that she had set up at home and had taught Carly all about photography as she grew up. Her mom may not have passed her love of history on to Carly, but she had bequeathed her skill in photography.

Serena stood in front of the dorm door while Carly focused her 35-millimeter camera. She moved back and refocused. Then she posed Serena with her hockey stick, counted to three and pushed the button. The camera buzzed softly and then stopped.

"All that for nothing," said Serena, shaking her head. "Now you'll have to wait until you get home to even see the picture."

"But at least I've got a good, clear shot to remember our arrival by."

"Maybe," acknowledged Serena. "But with my Polaroid, I always capture far more of everything as it's happening. And I can see it immediately. Besides, you never know what you might capture on film that you hadn't planned on."

Inside the dorm, a woman with a clipboard in her hand greeted them. After Serena and Carly gave their names, she directed them to the adjoining lounge, where they had their pictures taken and identification cards made. She showed them how to swipe their cards in the ID reader to allow them to pass the security desk and into the rest of the dorm. As she gave them their room number and handed them each a map of the dorm and the campus, she told them to meet in the dining hall at five o'clock. They'd receive their practice schedules and other information then.

Serena, Carly, and Mrs. Ritchie rode the elevator to the fifth floor and headed down a hall, the girls dragging their bags behind them.

"This is it," said Carly. "Room 512." She fumbled with the key for a second and then shoved it into the keyhole.

"Awesome!" exclaimed Serena, after Carly had flung the door open. She dropped her bags and hopped onto a bed, bouncing up and down. "Mattresses are okay. Which bed do you want?"

"I'll take the other one since you've already deformed the springs in that one."

"Touché!" said Serena, continuing to bounce.

"This is a nice room," commented Mrs. Ritchie.

Serena and Carly inspected their dressers, desks, and closets. Serena pulled back the drapes and peered out the window. "Look!" she exclaimed suddenly. "There's a train or trolley or whatever you call them going by."

"It's called the T," explained Mrs. Ritchie "which stands for 'transit' and is part of the Massachusetts Bay Transportation System. Most of the rail lines are underground, but parts of them run on the surface."

"I hope we get to ride on the subway," said Serena. "It looks like fun."

"It sounds creepy to me," said Carly, "riding on a train in a big hole under the ground."

The girls made up their beds with sheets and pillowcases they'd brought from home. Then Serena, as though performing a ceremonial ritual, carefully placed Bun-Bun and Mr. Monkey on her pillow like royalty on their thrones. The girls put their clothes into the dresser drawers—Serena stuffing and Carly making neat piles—and Serena dumped her goalie bag in the closet.

A short time later, Mrs. Ritchie said good-bye to the girls. "I need to swing by the Beacon Hill neighborhood and shoot some film of the old colonial homes for a colleague doing an article on American architecture," she explained. "The late afternoon sunlight will be just right. See you in two weeks, girls."

"Bye, Mom," said Carly.

"Thanks for the ride, Mrs. Ritchie," Serena said.

"I guess we better get to the dining room," said Carly after her mom had left. "It's almost five."

"Where is the dining hall?" asked Serena.

"I think the three dorms share two dining rooms. One of them is in Sleeper," said Carly, who was combing her hair and putting on a fresh shirt for dinner.

As they headed down the hall to the elevator, they met up with two other girls. "Hi," said Serena. "Are you guys here for hockey camp?"

"Yeah," said one girl, who had her hair in a headband. "I'm Beth, and this is my roommate, Haley."

"Hi," said Haley. She stood six feet tall, and Serena felt small in her presence.

"Where are you guys from?" asked Carly.

"Connecticut," said Haley.

"And I'm from New York," Beth answered.

After Serena and Carly had introduced themselves and explained they were both from Bar Harbor, Maine, they discovered that Beth and Haley were in room 502, just a few rooms down from theirs.

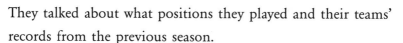

They talked about what positions they played and their teams'
records from the previous season.

When they arrived in the dining hall, they joined the other
field hockey players sitting at a group of tables. Ms. Shughart,
the woman with the clipboard, explained the dorm rules. Yelling
and loud radios were not allowed, lights had to be off at eleven
o'clock, and they should conduct themselves as ladies.

Ms. Rivera, one of the camp's instructors and a former U. S.
team player, discussed the practice sessions and scrimmages that
were planned. She passed out schedules to all the girls and
expressed her hope that they would work hard during their two
weeks of camp. Then she yelled, "Chow time," and the throng
of girls moved en masse to the food line.

While Serena and Carly and Beth and Haley waited in line,
they chatted with each other about their drives into Boston. Beth
howled at her three friends' excited description of the trains.
Haley, like Serena and Carly, lived in a small community and
was in awe of the city as much they were. Beth, on the other
hand, was from New York City. Subways and other public
transportation were a way of life for her.

Suddenly, a hush fell over the dining room as a large group of
boys entered. The words "basketball players" were whispered up
and down the cafeteria line and from table to table.

The four girls found a table at the far end of the room and
sat down. Before they had finished their salads, though, two
basketball players approached them.

"Can we sit here?" asked one. "The other seats are all taken."

The girls looked around at the completely filled tables and several boys standing with trays, desperately searching for a spot at which to sit.

"Sure," said Serena.

"It looks like they overbooked the dining hall flight," laughed Beth.

"I'm Derek," said the first boy, as he pulled out a chair.

"I'm Jon, his roommate," said the other.

The girls introduced themselves, and they all shared where they were from. Derek was from Harrisburg, the capital of Pennsylvania, and Jon lived in a town in New Jersey that none of the others had ever heard of.

After the other girls had told the boys their hometowns, Serena said, "I live in Bar Harbor now, but my dad was in the Navy, so I've lived all over. His first assignment was in the Philippines. He met my mom at a base dance. They dated during his two years stationed there, and, against her parents' wishes, married and came to the United States."

"How is it you ended up in Bar Harbor? There's no navy base there, is there?" asked Beth.

Serena explained about her dad's retirement from the navy and boat purchase and her mom's painting skill and how those had led them to the coastal tourist town and their current occupations.

"What do your parents do?" Serena asked Derek.

"My mom's an accountant, and my dad's a police detective in Harrisburg," he answered.

The rest of the dinner discussion centered around robberies and how evidence is gathered at a crime scene. Beth said that detectives frequented her neighborhood, asking folks about a robbery here or a shooting there.

Serena found detective work fascinating. She loved reading mysteries, especially ones in which teens like her investigated and solved crimes. Even though they were a little outdated, she'd read many of the Nancy Drew and Hardy Boys mysteries as well as others. As she read each book, she always tried to find the clues and solve the puzzles long before the author revealed the answers.

She even used to pretend she was a detective. Every time her family moved to a new base, she would enter her new house and search for clues left behind from the previous family. A Barbie shoe and the wheel from a toy car indicated a family with kids, and fur in the corner where the vacuum had missed was definite proof of a family cat.

As the group left the dining hall, they agreed to meet for breakfast. Then the boys continued on to Rich Hall, and the girls returned to the fifth floor. Serena and Carly hung out in Beth and Haley's room, chatting about a variety of things and getting better acquainted.

At ten o'clock, the girls returned to their room. Carly announced she was tired and started getting ready for bed.

As she gathered her towel, soap, and toothbrush, she looked at Serena. "Aren't you coming to bed?"

"Yeah. Later. I'm going down to watch the news first."

"You're kidding."

"You know I always watch the news," she answered. "It's history in the making."

"But lights are out at eleven," Carly reminded her.

"So I'll skip the sports report. I'll be in the room on time."

In the dorm's lounge, Serena got comfortable on a flowered couch and flipped on the local news. The world news was first, and then a story appeared about a city official who was suspected of stealing money from the city treasury account.

"Jason McElwee, Boston's assistant city treasurer, was questioned today about the disappearance of almost a hundred thousand dollars over the past two years," announced the reporter. "Detectives are investigating the case and talking with his associates."

For a couple of seconds, the camera showed a bewildered Mr. McElwee sitting at his desk and talking on the phone while police entered his office.

"Wow," said Serena out loud as she turned off the TV. "That sounds like some of the detective mysteries I've read. I wonder if Derek's dad has ever worked on a case like this? I sure hope the Boston detectives can get some answers."

CHAPTER FOUR

An Overactive Imagination

 The alarm pierced the air with its high-pitched scream. Serena moaned and pushed her hair off her face. She opened her eyes just far enough to squint at the portable alarm clock Carly had set on the dresser. "Carly," she croaked, "why did you set the alarm so early?"

"Early?" Carly answered. "It's seven o'clock. We have to be at breakfast by eight."

"Good," Serena muttered. "I can sleep another forty-five minutes."

"Maybe you need to skip your late night news reports and go to bed earlier," Carly suggested.

"Can't," mumbled Serena, rolling over.

Thirty minutes later the whirring of Carly's hair dryer roused Serena. After grunting a few more times, Serena kicked off the sheet and rolled to a sitting position.

"If you aren't ready by 7:55, I'm going to the dining hall without you," announced Carly.

Ten minutes later, Serena was back from her shower. She threw on a T-shirt and shorts, then pulled on her socks and stuck her feet in her sneakers. Grabbing an elastic, she wound her hair into a ponytail. She booted her wet towel across the floor with perfect goalie skill, though nearly kicking off her untied sneaker in the process, and raced out the door behind Carly.

"Hi, everyone," she said as she greeted their new friends in the dining hall. She and Carly set down their trays and pulled out chairs between Beth and Derek. Jon and Haley, sitting across from them, returned their greetings.

"Do you know your hair is dripping water down your back?" asked Jon.

"Oh," said Serena. She squeezed her ponytail, and water trickled off the end and onto her shirt, soaking the middle of her back. "I didn't have time to dry it."

"Yeah, right," said Carly. "She only got up fifteen minutes ago."

Serena and Carly ate cereal and juice and toast with jelly and talked with the others about the day's practices and drills and scrimmages they'd face. Shortly before nine, the boys left for the gym, and the girls gathered their hockey sticks, cleats, and water bottles. Carly grabbed one end of Serena's goalie bag and helped her lug it down to the field.

"It's gonna be hot today," said Beth.

"Tell me about it," said Serena. "I heard on the news last night that it's going to reach ninety degrees. It'll feel like a hundred and ninety with all my goalie equipment on."

The girls reached the field and joined the appropriate groups to practice dribbling and driving and other skills. Serena and the other goalies met at the circle in front of the goal cage for specific instruction on defending the cage. Ms. Shughart, minus her clipboard, put on goalie gear and demonstrated several saves they could practice.

Next, a group of players lined up in front of the cage to practice their shots on goal, providing the goalies a chance to practice saves as well. Beth was in this group, and she scored a goal on each goalie. All the girls, used to ground and grass, were astounded at the speed at which the balls rocketed across the smooth, flat, artificial turf.

Then it was Serena's turn. "You won't get past me," she said. She watched Beth dribble the ball back and forth, back and forth, then drive it towards the far corner of the cage. Serena dove for the ball and smacked it away with her glove. She shot her arms up in the air in victory. Beth smiled and gave her a thumbs-up.

"Nice save," she said. "But I'll get you next time."

Carly and Haley were in the next group. Serena proudly informed them of her success against Beth, but Haley just smiled. When it was her turn, she whacked the ball right between Serena's feet.

"I never even saw the ball!" exclaimed Serena.

"I did," Carly laughed. "It sailed right between your shoes."

"Touché," replied Serena.

Soon it was lunchtime, and the girls eagerly returned to the air conditioning of the dorm. They stopped at the bathroom, and Carly glanced in the mirror. Her eyes bulged as she saw the redness of her face.

"Aaahh!" she screeched. "I forgot to put on sunblock this morning!"

Beth and Haley stared at her, but Serena gave her an understanding smile. She'd witnessed Carly's pale, freckled skin burn and peel numerous times. It was never a pretty sight.

After lunch, they returned to the field for more drills. By mid-afternoon, they were dripping with sweat and welcomed a break. The girls gathered under some pine trees, and Carly moved every few minutes, making sure she stayed in the shade. She reapplied sunblock twice and kept checking under her shirtsleeves to see how severe the contrast was between her covered skin and the rest of her arms.

Serena had peeled off her goalie gear and was relaxing on her back, hoping her shirt would dry a bit before she had to pile on her equipment again. She stared at the clouds overhead as she flapped her shirt, trying to create a breeze. One cloud resembled a boat, and Serena suddenly wondered what was going on back home on the *Marta* and inside Maine-ly Paintings. Another cloud first looked like a car but then shifted into the shape of a cat. Serena smiled as she thought of Tux and how much he

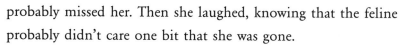

probably missed her. Then she laughed, knowing that the feline probably didn't care one bit that she was gone.

"Earth to Serena," said Carly.

Serena jumped. "Huh?"

"It's time to scrimmage," said Carly.

Serena groaned as she sat up, her damp shirt stuck fast to her back. She crawled back into her goalie gear and lumbered to the end of the field, pulling on her gloves as she stomped along. She watched the coaches divide the girls into teams. Carly and Haley were on her team, but Beth lined up in the middle of the field for the opposing side.

The playing was intense, and Serena found it difficult to concentrate with sweat rolling down her face in small rivers, cascading off her nose and chin. She licked the salty drops off her lips as she stared at the sky, hoping for a cloud. She saw one moving slowly and again its shape reminded her of the *Marta*. This time, though, Serena didn't wonder what her dad was doing on the boat. This time she imagined herself on the boat, facing into the stiff ocean breeze, the cold spray stinging her face, feeling wonderful.

"Heads up, Serena!" screamed Haley.

Serena looked up just in time to see Beth descending on her. But Serena's concentration and timing were off. Beth whacked the ball, and by the time Serena kicked her foot towards it, the ball had already thudded into the back of the cage.

"Gotcha!" Beth yelled.

"Nice one," said Serena.

"What on earth were you doing?" asked Haley. "You weren't even paying attention."

"I was sailing," she answered.

"You were what?"

"I know," Carly explained. "She was probably daydreaming about being at home on her dad's boat. Right?"

Serena gave her a perturbed you-know-me-too-well look.

After practice Serena finally made her daydream become real, at least partly anyway. Although the shower stall didn't look much like her dad's boat, with her overactive imagination, which Carly frequently teased her about, and the water turned to the coldest setting, she could just about believe it was ocean spray.

With her hair dripping just as it had for breakfast, she and Carly joined the others for dinner.

"I'll bet I know where you're from," laughed Jon, as he saw Carly, even though he knew she and Serena were from Maine. "You'd blend right in with the lobsters."

"Don't make jokes," chided Serena.

Carly felt her scarlet forehead. "I think I'm on fire." She picked up her glass of milk as well as Haley's and pressed them against each cheek, which were almost the color of the spaghetti sauce they were eating.

The group talked excitedly about the first day of camp. Derek and Jon described their brilliant playing and strategy. Derek demonstrated the three-point basket he had made with his balled-up napkin. It landed in the middle of a girl's plate at the table next to them, and they all doubled over with laughter as Derek retrieved it and apologized.

"Hey," said Beth to the boys after Derek was seated again. "Are you guys going on the field trip on Saturday?"

"To Fenway Park, Paul Revere's house and the Tea Party Ship?" asked Derek.

"Yeah," answered Serena, eagerly. "I can't wait."

The other girls stared at Serena, wide-eyed.

"You're joking, right?" asked Beth.

"No, I'm not," answered Serena. "Boston is a wonderful, historic city, and I'm glad I'm going to see some of it."

Now the boys stared at her as well. Carly laughed and explained to them Serena's strange love of history. "You should have heard her and my mom on the way down here. All they talked about was history and artifacts."

"I do have other interests," said Serena.

"Such as?" asked Beth.

"Mysteries and trying to solve them," she answered. She turned to Derek. "Tell us some more about your dad's detective work," she requested.

"Like what do you want to know?"

"Last night on the news—yes, I watch the news," she said before any of them could poke fun at her, "there was a story about a city official who police think stole a bunch of money from the city treasury. How would your dad solve a robbery like that?"

"That's not really a robbery," said Derek. "That's more of an embezzlement crime or an illegal transfer of funds type of thing."

"How would he go about investigating it?" asked Carly.

"Well, he'd check out the person—you know, like his background and stuff and maybe interview co-workers. He also looks for connections between people and the crime, something that might link the person to the stolen money or whatever."

"Then they arrest the person and put him in jail, right?" asked Haley.

"The justice system doesn't move that fast," said Serena. "They don't press charges on someone unless they're pretty sure the prosecutors can make it stick."

"You're right," agreed Derek. "My dad has to be able to prove there actually was a crime committed and have some pretty good evidence to support his theories about who committed the crime and why."

Later that evening, as Carly got ready for bed, Serena headed downstairs to view the day's news. She decided to write a letter to her family while she watched, the day's clouds of boats and cats triggering her desire, perhaps a need, to feel connected to home.

In the lounge, she sat, actually half lay, on the couch with a notebook propped up on her knee. She heard the weather report and was enormously glad to hear that the next day would be a little cooler. Then a reporter provided an update on the assistant city treasurer. Serena glanced up from her letter in time to see him being led away in handcuffs, holding his suit jacket over his face.

She returned to her letter and finished it a few minutes later. Since it was almost eleven, she knew she needed to get back to the room. As she headed for the TV to turn it off, the newsman began his final story.

"Employees at the Old North Church Museum discovered earlier today that a vial of original tea collected from the boot of one of the Boston Tea Party participants is missing. Police are investigating, but they're asking anybody who has been at the museum in the past few days and saw anyone or anything suspicious to notify authorities."

Serena froze in her steps, barely able to comprehend what she'd just heard. A moment later, a dorm chaperone appeared and scolded her for being up past curfew. As Serena hurried back to her room, her lips pursed and forehead wrinkled, she wondered how someone could manage to steal such an important historical artifact. But more importantly, who would steal it and why?

CHAPTER FIVE

Stolen Artifacts

 The next morning, Serena was ready for breakfast early with her hair toweled and even her shoes tied. She wanted as much time as possible to talk to Derek about the robbery of the tea she'd heard about on the news.

When the rest of their friends joined Serena and Carly, Serena filled them in on the missing tea. "How would your dad solve a crime like that?" she asked.

"Well," Derek chuckled. "I don't think my dad's ever been on this kind of case before. I mean, it's not like Harrisburg is the hot spot for historical artifacts."

"But how would he go about investigating a missing valuable?" she persisted. "In the detective books I've read, the police first look for clues left behind by the thief."

Derek nodded. "Yeah. He'd examine the crime scene and look for clues, but he'd also check to see if something else was missing or out of place." Derek paused, thinking. "He'd also try to determine if the thief had any help in committing the crime."

"An accomplice," said Serena.

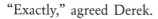

"Exactly," agreed Derek.

"And wouldn't he try to figure out the motive?" asked Jon.

"Duh. Robberies are generally committed with money in mind, I believe," said Beth, jokingly.

"Yeah, but stealing tea doesn't fit a money motive," said Haley, in Jon's defense.

"Maybe the thief was desperate for a finely aged cup of tea," suggested Beth. The group laughed so hard at this idea that the kids at the tables nearby stopped eating and stared at them.

That night Serena watched the news as usual, hoping for further information on the missing tea, but there wasn't any. The next day offered nothing new either. By Thursday, breakfast and dinner conversations turned away from crime solving and to letters and care packages from home. Jon had received a couple dozen homemade chocolate-chip-oatmeal cookies from his dad, a baker in a grocery store. He shared them with the others at dinner, each pigging out on four apiece.

Carly had received letters from both her mom and dad, and Serena was thrilled to find an envelope written in her father's handwriting. But nothing could surpass the letter she received Friday . . . from Tux. Maddie had penned the letter, of course, and Serena knew that by writing as Tux, Maddie would never have to admit to missing her sister by writing her own letter.

In the letter, Tux recounted his adventure in the weedy field nearby where he'd found a mouse, played with it until it died, and then deposited it in a box on Serena's bed for her to see when she got home. Serena groaned, realizing that maybe Maddie didn't miss her at all and that the letter was simply an attempt to bug her, making her wonder through the rest of camp if she would, indeed, return to this prize on her bed. To be safe, she decided she'd write to her mom and suggest she check her room. Her mom would thank her and yell horribly at Maddie if she did find Tux's smelly souvenir.

By Saturday morning, Serena and her friends were more than ready for a couple of days to relax and rest their tired muscles. Carly said she was just looking forward to some time out of the sun. After they'd all eaten a huge breakfast, Carly, Serena, and their friends boarded a school bus. Serena and Carly sat together, and Beth and Haley grabbed the seat behind them. Derek and Jon filled the seat in front.

Their tour guide boarded, introduced herself as Claire, and listed the places they would be touring. As the bus pulled away from the curb, Serena pulled out her Polaroid camera. She aimed it at Beth and pushed the button. The camera whirred and a second later spit out a square of plastic and paper. Serena peeled off the top layer and stared at the square. After Beth's picture slowly appeared, she passed it around to the others.

"What's with the Polaroid camera?" Haley whispered into Carly's ear. "I didn't think anybody used those anymore."

"You do if you're Serena and you want instant pictures of everything," she said.

"I heard that," said Serena. She quickly shot a picture of

their startled faces.

"Our first attraction," announced Claire as the bus eased away from the curb, "is the CITGO sign. I'm sure you've all seen it by now since at sixty square feet it's sort of hard to miss. It was built in 1965," she said "and contains over ten thousand feet of red, white, and blue neon tubing to light it up. During the energy crisis in the 1970s it was turned off and it was almost torn down in 1982. But the public rallied and eventually persuaded CITGO to keep it plugged in and maintained."

Their bus traveled the few blocks to Fenway Park, the stadium home for the Boston Red Sox baseball team. As they drove alongside the turquoise-colored structure nestled among city streets, Claire explained that it was built in 1912 and then rebuilt in 1935. "It's the smallest major-league park in the country and actually has real grass, not fake turf. How many of you are planning to take in the game next Saturday?"

Every boy's hand on the bus flew into the air.

"That's what I expected," Claire laughed. "Next stop is the Boston Common and the Public Garden."

The bus wound through city streets. Traffic was heavy even though it was Saturday, and Serena laughed to herself as she realized she hadn't escaped tourist traffic after all. A short time later a large area of trees and other greenery appeared, and the bus slowed to a stop.

"This is the Common," said Claire, "called that because it originally was designed for common use as a cow pasture. A cow hasn't grazed here, though, since 1830. The city later turned it into a park, and it's the oldest public park in the country."

Serena and Carly and the others followed Claire off the bus and onto the sidewalk. Just down the street stood a small visitors' center announcing information and maps for the Freedom Trail, which began in front of the building. Serena found the red bricks imbedded in the sidewalk and couldn't wait to come back the next Saturday and walk the path, visiting each and every historic site along the way.

They followed a path into the Common, dodging throngs of other people, locals and tourists alike, all out to enjoy the city's wooded oasis. Serena aimed her camera and snapped pictures of joggers running by, sweating profusely. After these had developed, she searched for other sights to shoot that would capture a typical day on the Common.

She aimed at fathers with video cameras recording their wives and children feeding the squirrels. Further down the path, she snapped pictures of folks crowding the benches, some talking with each other and others sipping coffee while reading their newspapers.

Serena marveled at the other sights around her. A vendor and his cart stood near the T entrance offering Boston shirts, hats, and mugs for sale.

"Try to stay together," called Claire above the wail of a police car siren. "We'll walk through the Common and then across the street to the Public Garden."

"Is that a pond up there?" asked Derek, as they started down a path.

"It's called the Frog Pond," answered Claire, "even though there are no frogs in it. I guess there was a real frog pond here long ago, but now it's just a man-made pond for waders in the summer and skaters in the winter."

"Oh, I wish we could go wading," said Haley.

"Same here," agreed Jon. "My feet are sweating."

"What are you taking a picture of, Carly?" asked Derek.

Everyone watched Carly fasten a long lens onto her camera. "There's the cutest toddler in the far end of the pond." She pointed, and they followed the line of her finger until they saw a little girl in denim overalls, no shirt, pant legs rolled up and blond curls bouncing around her face. Carly focused and stood perfectly still, waiting. Just as the little girl bent over to splash the water, Carly snapped the picture. "Got it!" she said triumphantly.

The group continued on, listening to Claire, and followed her into the Public Garden. She led them straight to a much larger pond with a footbridge crossing the middle. Ducks quacked from on the water and along the edge, and children fed them corn.

"Look at the swans!" exclaimed Serena.

"What swans?" asked Jon. "All I see are ducks."

"The swan boats," clarified Carly. "They're gorgeous."

After getting permission from Claire, all the girls ran over to the boat dock and waited for a swan boat to return. Carly photographed one of the huge, white, fiberglass birds sitting atop a green and red boat as it slowly moved towards them. After several families exited the boat, the girls stepped on, along with a dozen others. The boat operator in the back began cycling the pedals, and the boat glided through the lagoon.

"This is so cool!" said Beth excitedly.

"Haven't you ever been on a paddleboat before?" asked Serena.

"There isn't exactly a pond on every corner in my New York neighborhood."

"Serena, I'll bet you feel like you're on your father's boat on the ocean," said Haley, kiddingly.

"Oh, yes," agreed Serena, "and the waves are so rough." She rocked her body back and forth, as if from the motion of waves on the lake. "I'm not sure I can take much more. In fact, I feel . . . I feel . . . like I'm going to barf!" Serena made a retching noise and pretended to throw up into an imaginary bag.

Carly rolled her eyes and shook her head while the others wrinkled their noses and laughed at the awful picture Serena had created for them. The pedaler ignored the girls and continued pedaling the boat on around the lagoon and back to the dock. The fifteen-minute trip was much too short.

After a brief stop at a statue of George Washington at the far end of the garden, Claire led the group along more winding paths and stopped at one of Boston's most famous garden statues, bronze likenesses of Mrs. Mallard and her eight ducklings, a bit larger than life size.

"This mother duck and her ducklings are the heroes of the children's book *Make Way for Ducklings*," Claire explained. "Are all of you familiar with the story?"

Most knew the story, but a few had never heard it.

"The book, by Robert McCloskey," recounted Claire, "tells how Mrs. Mallard stopped traffic on Beacon Street as she and her ducklings marched across the road to the garden to meet up with Mr. Mallard at the lagoon."

As Claire talked, noisy children patted the ducks, sat on them, and hugged them. Other children waddled nearby, flapping their arms and quacking, their parents furiously taking pictures and videos of them. Some of the children even threw corn at the ducks.

"You might find it hard to believe," said Claire, "but two ducklings have been stolen since the statue was first placed here in 1987. In 1989 Mack was stolen and, through a local fundraising campaign, was replaced. And then ten years later, Jack disappeared. Fortunately, he showed up a couple of weeks later in the library at nearby Boston College. Authorities believe some college kids took him as a prank," Claire said.

"At least they were able to put it back," Beth said.

"Actually," said Claire, "the duck's leg was so damaged when it was wrenched off that he couldn't be fastened back on properly.

That duck is now part of a display to entertain sick children at the Boston Medical Center. This is a new duck."

"Who'd want a duck statue in their house anyway?" asked Derek.

"It would certainly be a great souvenir of Boston," suggested Serena, chuckling. "Better than the faded lobster traps tourists buy in Maine."

"But really, except as a prank, why would someone steal one of these ducks?" asked Jon.

"Because it's so symbolic of Boston," announced Serena, serious all at once, having suddenly realized a financial motive for stealing something like the duck—or tea from the ship. "Owning a piece of the city would be an honor among certain collectors. There must be a lot of folks who would pay a lot of money for things like this."

CHAPTER SIX

Underneath the City

 It was soon time for lunch and Claire led her tour group back towards the bus.

"Are we headed the right way?" Serena muttered to Carly. "Shouldn't we have taken that path over there?"

Carly stared at her. "Only if you wanted to end up on the opposite side of the Common from the bus."

Serena frowned. "I thought the bus was over that way." She pointed to a path leading off to the right.

Carly laughed. "You always get turned around and lost."

"I do not," protested Serena.

"Are you forgetting the time you went with us to Portland and we stayed in that hotel? You got lost on your way back from the ice machine."

"It was a big hotel," countered Serena.

"Or the time I went camping with you," continued Carly. "We had to go looking for you when you didn't come back from the bathroom. You were wandering around in another whole part of the campground."

"Well . . . it was dark, and one group of trees looks like another."

Carly smiled at Serena but said nothing more since they had reached the bus. They grabbed a brown bag lunch from a box and a soda from a cooler and joined the other kids under a tree. Between bites, Serena snapped pictures of the squirrels that darted up to the kids and nabbed the bits of bread tossed their way. She was amazed at how tame they were.

When they'd finished lunch, they boarded the bus for the drive across the city to Paul Revere's house.

"I don't think I'd ever want to drive on these narrow streets," said Carly, peering out the window. "There's barely six inches between the bus and the parked cars."

"That's why Boston has a reputation as one of the worst cities in the country to drive in," said Claire, overhearing Carly's comment. "The north end, where we're headed, is a maze of very narrow streets that run in all directions with no organized layout. I've lived here all my life, and I never drive in the old part of the city, or in much of any of the city, because the roads are so confusing. Most Bostonians make good use of the subway system, which we'll ride on from the Paul Revere House to the Boston Tea Party Ship."

Near Paul Revere's house, Claire led the group up a cobblestone street to a gray clapboard building. After passing through a gate in a high brick wall, they found themselves in an herb garden. Throngs of people stood around, waiting their turn to tour the house once occupied by the city's most famous messenger. While they waited, Carly positioned all her friends in front of a plot of herbs and got a group picture with her camera.

Serena couldn't wait to go inside and view her first historical artifacts of Boston. She intended to commit each one to memory since they might come in handy for a future history report on some aspect of colonial life.

When it was their group's turn, Serena stepped over the threshold, feeling like she was entering a time machine transporting her back to the 1770s. A tour guide dressed in colonial clothes led them into the kitchen. Along a railing that separated the area of artifacts from the rest of the room were plaques bearing information about the kitchen. Serena stopped to read each one.

"How many children did Paul Revere have?" asked a man near her.

"Sixteen," answered the guide. Several people gasped.

"Is it true that he made false teeth for George Washington?" asked Serena, remembering reading something about it in last year's history book.

The costumed woman smiled. "It's believed that he did, but it's never been confirmed."

While Serena listened to the other questions and answers, she stared at every artifact and antique in the kitchen. A bellows, used to fan the fire in the enormous brick fireplace, rested on the mantle. A black iron kettle hung inside the fireplace on a hook.

Next to the fireplace stood an antique popcorn popper and a candle mold.

After passing through the sitting room adjoining the kitchen, the girls navigated the narrow spiral staircase to the master bedroom, which boasted a flowered canopy bed. Serena quickly turned her attention, though, to a locked glass case that stood in one corner. She gazed in awe at the artifacts inside, barely able to believe she was actually looking at Paul Revere's reading glasses and walking stick, Rachel Revere's ring, and a letter signed by Mr. Revere himself.

There was even an old book containing Henry Wadsworth Longfellow's famous 1861 poem, "Paul Revere's Ride," which she'd read in English class a couple of years before. It recounted, somewhat inaccurately, his part in alerting the Minutemen of British troop movement, creating the legend everyone is familiar with.

"Oh, no," said Serena suddenly. "I forgot to take pictures." She turned to Carly. "I've got to go back to the kitchen. I'll be right back."

Carly sighed. "Just hurry up," she warned.

Serena returned to the kitchen, where another group had already begun their tour. The same female guide stood off to the side, talking with a man also in a colonial costume. Serena, pushed into a corner by the incoming tourists, aimed her camera as best she could and snapped a shot, imagining what a great picture she'd have of seemingly real colonial people in an authentic eighteenth-century kitchen.

As people milled about the room, Serena slid among the people towards the front. She took another picture, aimed again and shot one more.

"You aren't allowed to take photos inside the house," said the woman as she noticed Serena's camera.

"Oh, I'm sorry," Serena apologized. "I didn't know that."

"There's a sign on the door," said the colonial man, a bit gruffly. His eyebrows arched as he stared down at her.

Serena quickly slung her camera over her shoulder and headed through the hall and up the steps, rejoining Carly, who had moved into the back bedroom. When she saw the small bed, with a lumpy mattress supported only by ropes, she wondered how many of Paul Revere's sixteen children had shared it.

When they'd finished touring the house, they joined Claire and the others and walked the few blocks to the T station. After they marched down a flight of concrete steps into Boston's underground, Claire gave them each a gold token and they filed through the turnstiles one at a time. They followed Claire through an orange-painted hallway and onto the platform, where dozens of people stood around, some mingling and talking, others keeping to themselves, several holding packages, bouncing infants, or reading papers. It was a sea of humanity, each person uniquely different yet all gathered there for one common reason:

speedy transportation to where they wanted to go.

"It's sort of creepy down here," whispered Carly. "Like we're in a cave."

"Why are you whispering?" asked Serena.

"I don't know. It just feels like the kind of place where you need to keep your voice down," she answered.

Suddenly, the mournful tune of a saxophone rolled through the still air. Serena and Carly and the others walked a short way on the platform and found a man with grizzled whiskers sprouting from his face and a tam on his head playing his instrument for all he was worth. Dollar bills and change lined the open sax case sitting in front of him. As the kids watched him play, several people strolled up and pitched some change into it.

"He gets paid for playing?" asked Jon.

"Only if the people pay him," answered Claire. "Playing his saxophone in the subway is how he makes his living."

Carly and Serena stared at each other in disbelief. "Welcome to city life," mumbled Carly.

"Anyway," agreed Serena.

All at once the earth shook, and a deafening roar filled the tunnel. Serena strained her neck to see around the people, who suddenly moved like a gigantic wave towards the edge of the platform. Blazing headlights filled the tunnel as the T rounded a bend and slowed in front of them.

"Stay together on the train," yelled Claire above the noise. "We get off at Downtown Crossing—in case anyone gets separated."

"Separated?" questioned Serena. "Now there's a scary thought. How would you ever find your way back out of here?"

"All the train lines are color coded," said Carly. "See?" She opened up a map of the subway system she'd picked up on the way in. "You just follow the map."

"That map looks like a strange, multicolored spider to me," Serena said, frowning as she looked at the diagram of red, blue, orange, and green lines radiating out from a central square.

The doors of the train slid open by themselves, and Serena and Carly rushed in. Since all the seats were filled inside, they had to stand. Suddenly, the doors closed, and as if by some secret knowledge it possessed, the train lurched forward and sped into the dark tunnel ahead. Serena and Carly grabbed the metal railing attached to the seat beside them to avoid being pitched into the laps of those sitting in it.

The train raced through the dark, stopping at two other stations before the signs for Downtown Crossing came into view. When the doors slid open, the kids exited, followed Claire from the Orange Line to the Red Line, entered another train, and whizzed away towards South Station.

Back on the street, they blinked as their eyes adjusted to the afternoon sun. A short walk brought them to the Boston Tea Party Ship and Museum where they boarded the boat, a replica of one of the three ships loaded with tea that had docked at Griffin's Wharf in December 1773.

When it was their turn to tour the boat, a costumed guide informed them that they would be part of a tea party reenactment. First he incited the colonists into voicing their feelings regarding the high tax they were forced to pay on tea and other goods.

"Are we going to pay the king's tariff?" he shouted.

"No," several shouted. "Not any more."

"Are ye willing to protest, fellow colonists? Are ye ready to fight for your rights?"

Cheers erupted from the crowd as they rallied in their freedom fight.

"Now then," the guide continued, "I've come up with a plan. If the tea is destroyed, we do not have to pay the tax on it. So, I leave it to you good townspeople. How should we get rid of the tea?"

"Dump it!"

"But that would be an act of treason, punishable by hanging, if caught. Therefore, we will disguise ourselves as Indians so the soldiers can't recognize us."

He handed out Indian headdresses and feathers to the crowd. "Dump the tea!" he shouted.

"Into the sea!" responded Serena and Carly along with the others.

"Dump the tea!"

"Into the sea!"

Bales of tea were handed out, and everyone tossed a bundle defiantly over the side. Serena and Carly laughed along with everyone else as the guide pulled the tea, attached to the boat with a rope, back on board to prepare it for the next tour.

"That was the best yet," said Serena, reveling in the experience of what it might have been like on that night so long ago in the colonists' quest for freedom.

At the gift shop next door, Serena bought a small box of tea as a souvenir, not a real artifact but a suitable substitute. And she wondered anew what had happened to the tea stolen from the Old North Church Museum.

CHAPTER SEVEN

A Mysterious Photograph

When the group arrived back at the university, Serena and Carly traipsed slowly to their room to rest up a bit before dinner.

"I'm beat," said Carly, kicking off her shoes. "My feet are so sore, I'll need all day to rest tomorrow if there's to be any hope that I can run and dribble a ball down the field on Monday."

"I hear you," agreed Serena. She had flopped onto her bed and was busy propping Bun-Bun under her head for a pillow. Then she unzipped several plastic bags and started sorting through a huge stack of pictures.

"How many pictures did you take today?" Carly asked.

"I'm not sure. A lot anyway."

"Let's see some," Carly said. She grabbed a pile and began looking through it. "I really need to give you some lessons," she said after viewing several blurry shots that appeared to be close-ups of squirrels.

"Forget the squirrels," said Serena sharply, "and look at these." She rolled off of her bed and handed Carly some shots taken

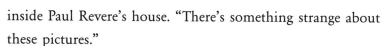
inside Paul Revere's house. "There's something strange about these pictures."

Carly stared at the pictures that Serena had handed her. "Exactly what am I supposed to see?" she asked.

"Look at the guides," she said, pointing to the man and woman. "When I took the picture, I really couldn't tell what the guides were doing since it was so crowded. But now that I've really looked at the photo, it looks like the woman is putting something into a bag. And look at the next one." Serena pointed to the second photo she'd taken. "Now she's handing the bag to the man."

"So what?" asked Carly.

Serena sighed loudly. "Don't you get it?" she said. "She's stealing an artifact and giving it to the other guide to get it out of the house."

"You're kidding, right?" Carly asked.

"I'd never make a joke about something historical," answered Serena.

"Well, I think you're imagining something that's not really there, like when you see things in the clouds. Besides, you can't tell from this photo that they're stealing something. She might have been handing the guide his lunch, for all you know."

"It isn't his lunch," said Serena. "And the man was sort of mean to me, like he was mad I'd taken a picture of him."

"I'd be mad, too," said Carly. "Especially since you told me that picture taking isn't allowed inside the house."

Serena ignored Carly's comment and began shuffling through the pictures again. She placed two side by side and studied them. Something seemed different between the pictures, but she couldn't figure out what. "Look!" she shouted, suddenly seeing, or rather not seeing something. "In the first picture, there's an antique candle mold next to the woman. And in the third one, it's gone."

Carly squinted at the picture. "Yeah, there's something there and then not there, but how can you tell it's a candle mold? The shot's so blurry."

"Because I'd looked at and memorized every artifact when I was in the kitchen the first time," answered Serena, "and I know it was a candle mold that was on the floor next to the popcorn popper."

"That doesn't mean it was stolen," she argued. "Maybe it was sent out to be polished."

"You don't polish artifacts," Serena said. "Mr. Cantwell said that would ruin their authenticity." She scooped up the small mountain of plastic squares and, after bundling them into groups with rubber bands, stuck them into a bag. She placed the three shots of Paul Revere's kitchen on the bottom of the pile. "I'm taking the pictures to dinner, and I'll ask the others what they think."

Serena and Carly were the first of their group in the dining hall. They found a table and put their trays down and then headed back to the salad bar. By the time they returned to the table, the others had arrived.

"What on earth is this stuff?" asked Beth as she stirred her spoon through a bowl filled with brown, oval beans in a sauce.

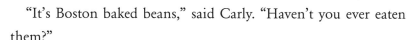

"It's Boston baked beans," said Carly. "Haven't you ever eaten them?"

"I've had canned franks and beans before," she answered, "but they didn't look anything like this."

"Boston's famous for its baked beans," explained Derek. "Its nickname is Beantown."

"Umm," said Beth after sampling some. "It's good."

"Are those your pictures from today, Serena?" asked Haley, spying the plastic bag on the table next to her.

Serena and Carly exchanged glances.

"Yeah, they are," Serena answered. She unzipped the bag and passed out several packs of pictures, careful to leave the bundle of three in the bag. She would save those for last.

Serena's friends passed around the pictures, laughing at the ones Serena had taken of them.

"What is this?" Haley asked.

Carly picked it up. "It's a close-up of a squirrel's tail."

The boys looked at the picture and exploded in laughter.

Serena knew it was time. "Well, maybe some of my shots aren't the best," she said. "But look at these." She passed out the three photos of the kitchen and waited.

"These look like Paul Revere's kitchen," said Beth.

"I thought you couldn't take pictures inside," Jon said.

"There was a sign on the door, I think," added Haley.

"Well, I missed the sign and went back to the kitchen to take some," said Serena impatiently. "Before I was told to stop, I'd gotten three pictures." She continued on, showing them first the photo with the candle mold and then the one with one guide passing the bag to the other. Finally she put the shot with the missing mold in front of them and explained her theory that it had been stolen.

"What's a candle mold anyway?" asked Derek.

"It's the metal form the colonial people poured wax into to make candles," explained Serena.

"But why would somebody steal it?" questioned Beth.

"Well, it's not like there are a bunch of these around today. They're antiques, and this one might even date to the 1770s, making it especially rare," Serena explained.

"I think you've got an overactive historical imagination," said Jon.

"That's what I told her," Carly said.

Derek nodded. "You have to be careful with assumptions, Serena," he said. "Maybe some tea was stolen, but you can't just assume the candle mold has also been stolen. You need solid proof that it was stolen, not just a fuzzy picture and a wild hunch."

The others nodded silently in agreement.

Serena collected her pictures, shaking her head. She would never get the others to believe her. But she did realize that some further evidence would go a long way towards convincing them of her theory.

That night she watched the news on TV as usual. She was alone in the dorm lounge as she listened to the local Boston news, hoping to hear a report about a candle mold being stolen from Paul Revere's house. There wasn't one. There was no report the next night either.

By Monday morning, Serena was beginning to believe that maybe her imagination had run away with her. Surely an antique from one of Boston's most important historical sites would have been missed and reported by now. Though not giving up on her theory altogether, Serena decided to put her focus and energy into her hockey playing.

The second week on the hockey fields, to Serena's relief, was cooler. She still sweltered inside her goalie gear, but she sweated less, enabling her to concentrate better. Concentration alone, though, wasn't enough to keep Beth, Haley, and Carly from each scoring on her. She made lots of good saves, however, and Coach Rivera complimented her several times, telling her she had the potential to be a great high school goalie.

Carly, on the other hand, was not faring as well. Her sunburn intensified each day with additional exposure to the sun, even though she'd slathered sunscreen all over her body. A nurse at the university's medical clinic had given her some zinc ointment, which she'd covered her nose and ears with, the white cream causing some strange looks from people. By Friday, she'd begun to peel on her face, neck, and arms, the dead skin flaking off in thin layers resembling tissue paper.

"I can't wait to go shopping tomorrow," said Carly to the other girls as they walked from the practice field back to the dorm on Friday afternoon. "I can spend the whole day inside and out of the sun."

"I've been saving babysitting money all summer," said Haley, "just so I can shop at Filene's Basement."

"You're going to shop in a basement?" asked Serena.

"Serena, you know as much about shopping as we do about history," said Beth, laughing. "Filene's Basement is a famous Boston store that holds these incredible sales."

"You can buy stuff at 75 percent off!" said Haley. "I'm going to buy some Christmas gifts since I'll be able to get things really cheap."

"Are you guys planning to spend your whole free day in Boston shopping?" asked Serena.

"Aren't you?" asked Beth.

"No way," she answered. "I'm walking the Freedom Trail." Serena saw their blank looks and had to explain the historical path through Boston.

"Well, you're going to be walking alone," said Haley. "Everyone I've talked to is going shopping somewhere, or to the game at Fenway."

"So I'll go alone," said Serena stubbornly. "I'm not spending two weeks in Boston without visiting all the historic sites."

As the evening wore on, though, Serena began to think that maybe she should go with her friends since Saturday would be the last day to spend with them. On Sunday, after several final games, everyone would be going home.

At ten-thirty, she said goodnight to Carly and headed to the lounge to watch the news, still mulling over what she should do the next day. Sprawled on a couch, she only half listened to the day's world events and the news about local happenings.

Suddenly, the word *duck* interrupted her thoughts, and she bolted upright.

"We join Jesse Anders, who was at the Public Garden this afternoon when the duck was reported stolen," the anchorman was saying.

"This is Jesse Anders," said the on-site reporter, "here at the bronze statues of Mrs. Mallard and her eight ducklings, only now there are seven. Early this morning, a policeman on his rounds discovered that one of the ducks is missing, probably the work of pranksters. Police are asking anyone with information on the duck's whereabouts to contact them."

Serena sat motionless. Had she heard correctly that now a duck was missing, too?

CHAPTER EIGHT

Smugglers in Boston

 It was several seconds before Serena could even react. Then she leaped from the couch and raced back to her room. Halfway there she remembered she'd forgotten to turn off the TV, so she ran back. When she finally arrived at her room, her chest was heaving and her pulse pounding. She flipped on the light and tried to catch her breath. "Carly?" she gasped. "Are you asleep?"

"Not anymore," Carly whined, her eyes barely open. "Turn off the light and go to bed."

Serena ignored her, and, having regained enough air in her lungs to speak again, frantically began retelling what she'd just heard on the news. "First some tea is missing, then the candle mold, and now one of Mrs. Mallard's ducks has disappeared. Someone is stealing artifacts from Boston, a collector or someone."

Carly covered her eyes from the overhead light and squinted up at Serena. "I still don't believe it," she said.

"Well, the duck didn't fly away on its own!" exclaimed Serena.

"But there still could be a logical explanation for why each item is missing. They might not necessarily be connected to each other."

Serena pondered this statement. "Then I'll have to prove that a connection exists," she concluded.

"Prove it?" questioned Carly. "Just report it to the police and let them handle it. I'm sure there are trained detectives in Boston who investigate disappearing stuff."

"The items didn't disappear. They were stolen by someone who knows the value of an artifact," she said conclusively. "And if I report my suspicions," Serena continued, "they'd never believe me. Not without proof."

"So show them your pictures," suggested Carly.

"Yeah, right," said Serena. "That ought to convince them, just like they convinced you and the others." She paused. "What I need are good pictures, like you take."

"But I didn't take any at Paul Revere's house," said Carly.

Serena stopped again, thinking how to best phrase her next suggestion so Carly would agree to it. She had been at this same point many times with Carly, like the time they'd hiked to Bar Island. She had climbed down on some rocks to wave to her dad as the *Marta* sailed by. While climbing back up the rocks, she had slipped and twisted her ankle.

Carly had wanted her to stay put while she went for help rather than risk further injury to her ankle. But she had convinced Carly she could walk back to the mainland. As a result, her mild ankle sprain had worsened considerably, landing her on crutches for two weeks. Serena grimaced at the memory.

Another time she'd persuaded Carly into believing that there was no hockey practice since it was a school holiday. They couldn't play in the next game because they'd missed the practice. And Serena could think of other incidences as well. She sighed and prepared herself for Carly's logical arguments against her plan.

She inhaled deeply and spoke in her calmest, most persuasive voice. "But we could walk the Freedom Trail, find that colonial man and woman again, and catch them stealing something else."

"You actually think we could find two people in one day among the throngs of tourists and other people on the streets of Boston?" asked Carly.

"Well, it's not like everybody is dressed in colonial clothes. They'd stand out. And besides, the only streets we need to check are on the Freedom Trail."

"But you don't know if they'll be on the trail," countered Carly.

"They're bound to be trying to steal things from other historical sites," argued Serena.

"So how will we know at which sites they'll be?"

"We'll just start at the beginning of the trail and walk from site to site. When we see them, we'll follow them and wait for them to make a move. If we see them do something suspicious, you take a good clear picture, we get the pictures developed, and we turn them in to the police. The smuggling ring is broken, and the artifacts returned."

"Now there's a smuggling ring?" asked Carly.

"Say you'll go with me," pleaded Serena. "We can even do some shopping at the stores in Faneuil Hall. There are supposed to be some good shops there and at North and South Markets."

"But I need a day out of the sun," argued Carly.

"The weatherman said it's to be cloudy tomorrow."

Then there was silence. Serena held her breath, hoping Carly was out of arguments.

"You win," Carly said, "but only if you promise to shop for school clothes with me when we get back home. That'll even the score a bit."

"Oh, all right," said Serena, realizing she'd have to agree to this condition, at least for now. She'd try to get out of it when they returned to Bar Harbor.

"Now let me get some sleep," said Carly.

But sleep didn't come easily for Serena. She was full of energy and tossed and turned on her bed, the sheets bunching under her, as her mind raced through her investigation plans. In desperation, she began counting sheep, trying to bore herself to sleep, but the sheep kept turning into bronze ducks, waddling across Beacon Street. Eventually, she drifted off.

In the morning, Serena dragged herself out of bed a full half hour before breakfast to ensure plenty of time to prepare for the day's investigation. Carly, however, was way ahead of her. She'd already showered and dressed and was busily laying out everything on her bed that she planned to take.

"Why are you taking all that stuff?" asked Serena as she watched Carly.

"Because I need it," she replied.

"Tissues? Band-Aids? A granola bar?" asked Serena, picking up the items one at a time.

"Suppose my sneakers begin to rub? I don't want to get a blister. And you know I always get hungry mid morning."

"Why the tissues? You don't have a cold."

Carly shrugged. "I always take them just in case."

Serena frowned as Carly packed these items into her backpack as well as sunscreen and her subway map and wallet. "How are you going to carry all that plus your camera bag with your lenses and stuff?"

"I'm not," answered Carly, grinning. "This is your idea, so you're carrying the camera bag."

Serena shrugged and hurried out the door for her shower. When she returned, she threw on shorts, shirt, socks, and sneakers. Next, she grabbed some money from her wallet and stuffed it into her shorts pocket.

"I'm ready," she said.

Carly threw her towel at her. "Would you please dry your hair first? You look like a drowned rat."

Serena briskly rubbed her head, pitched her towel in the direction of a chair, and followed Carly out the door.

"Do me a favor," said Carly as they rode the elevator down to the dining hall. Don't tell the others I've decided to go with you."

"Why not?"

"Because they'll think I'm nuts and try to talk me out of helping you with your silly plan, and they might succeed."

"I won't say a word," promised Serena.

At breakfast they endured conversations from the boys about the day's line-up, no-hitters, batting averages, and the possibility of catching an out-of-the-park, homerun ball during the game at Fenway. The girls discussed the line-up up of stores to shop in, including Carly in their discussion. She simply nodded in agreement. Serena was excluded from the start after she confirmed that she was, indeed, setting out on the Freedom Trail. But she honored Carly's request and didn't add that she would be going with her.

The dining hall began to empty as each table of students finished breakfast and headed out to the waiting buses. Serena grabbed an extra doughnut, wrapped it in a napkin, and stuck it in Carly's camera case, deciding Carly's preparedness in case of hunger was a good idea.

Two dorm supervisors met each student as they boarded the buses, wrote down where each planned to get off, and established a pick-up time later in the day. Serena whispered to one of the women that the Boston Common, the starting point of the Freedom Trail, was their destination. Looking amused, the supervisor whispered back that the bus would pick them up at 5:00.

The bus traveled towards its first stop, Fenway Park, where the streets had already begun to fill with sidewalk vendors selling hot dogs, cotton candy, lemonade, and peanuts as well as Red Sox pennants, caps, T-shirts, and water containers.

As the bus inched towards a stadium entrance gate, the boys' enthusiasm reached a crescendo. While they noisily exited the bus, one of the chaperones reminded them the bus would pick them up at exactly the same spot at 5:30. If the boys heard her, it wasn't apparent.

The half-full bus continued on the route they'd traveled the previous Saturday towards the Common and Garden, as the girls discussed the day's shopping itinerary. Some, like Beth and Haley, planned to shop at Filene's Basement. Others had opted to browse the finer, more upscale stores around Faneuil Hall. Almost all planned to look for clothes for themselves.

"Why are we stopping here?" Beth asked as the bus slowed to a stop alongside the entrance to the Common.

"Serena's being dropped off here for her history tour," answered Haley.

"Oh, yeah. I forgot."

As Carly stood up and then walked up the aisle after Serena, the other girls sat speechless.

"Carly!" exclaimed Beth, once her shock had passed. "How on earth did Serena talk you onto that stupid trail and out of Filene's Basement?"

Carly sighed loudly and looked at the other girls. "You wouldn't even believe it if I told you."

"We're on the trail of a missing duck!" exclaimed Serena, flapping her arms and quacking as she hopped down the steps. After looking back through the windows, she laughed at the girls' puzzled expressions. But then her smile faded and wrinkles formed on her forehead. Did she really think she could crack this case of missing artifacts?

Shadows in the Cemetery

As the bus pulled away, the girls gazed around them, attempting to orient themselves to their surroundings. It was a spectacular day, clear with low humidity. The air blew the leaves in the trees just enough to rustle them.

"I thought you said it would be cloudy," said Carly, already reaching for her sunscreen.

"Maybe it'll cloud up later," Serena suggested.

They'd been dropped near the Park Street subway station, the busy hub in the center of the city near the Boston Common and the Public Garden. A deafening roar filled the air, and Serena and Carly stuck their fingers in their ears. They looked up and saw a huge jet climbing through the sky, having just taken off from nearby Logan International Airport. Across the street two police officers mounted on horses chatted together.

Jazz music wafted out of a café and was carried on the breeze along with the smells of freshly brewed coffee and bagels. A tour bus, resembling an old-time Boston trolley, rolled slowly down the street. Every seat was filled with tourists straining to see the sights that their tour guide explained to them as they passed by. The girls maneuvered through the crowd of people, some hurrying, others strolling leisurely, and some at a complete stop, talking with friends.

Carly turned to Serena. "Let's stop in at the tourist information center," she said, pointing to the small brick building just down the street from the Common. "I want to get a map of the Freedom Trail."

"What for?" asked Serena. "All we do is follow the red bricks in the sidewalk from one historical site to another. See?" She pointed to the sidewalk, where a double line of red bricks was imbedded in the cement.

"Well, Mom said it was three miles long, and I'd just feel better if I knew where we were going," replied Carly.

Inside the information center, Carly picked up a map of the trail and of downtown Boston. Serena found a book explaining the history of the sites on the trail and decided to buy it so she could read about each place they stopped at.

The girls began at the first bricks in the sidewalk and followed the double row up the street through the Common and towards a large building with a huge, golden dome. Serena alternated between scanning the entries in her book and scanning the people passing by, staying alert for the colonial duo from the Paul Revere House.

"Is that the capitol?" asked Carly.

"Yes, but it's always called the State House," said Serena.

"Couldn't we skip it? I mean, do you really think someone is going to steal something from the State House?"

Serena shrugged. "I won't know until I see what's inside."

As the girls entered the building, they gawked at the floor with its thousands of one-inch-square tiles arranged in a variety of designs. Overhead, intricate stained glass panels were illuminated by the sun. Enormous paintings depicting important events in Massachusetts history filled the walls.

They joined a tour and followed the group into the room where the House of Representatives meets. In the back of the room hung a three-foot-long wooden fish complete with fins and suspended in mid-air by two wires.

"The Sacred Cod was presented to the legislature in 1784 by a Boston merchant," said the guide. "It's always hung in the House of Representatives, but in 1933 it was stolen as a prank and hidden in a closet downstairs."

"This must be some city for stealing stuff," Serena whispered to Carly. But the girls agreed it would be too hard to reach to take down and too awkward to sneak out of the building.

"The next stop is the Park Street Church and the Granary Burying Ground," said Serena when they returned to the street.

"Oh, sure. Someone dug up a body and took it home with them," Carly suggested.

"Actually," said Serena, "some famous gravestones have been stolen."

"Like whose?"

"Mother Goose's for one."

Carly stopped in her tracks and stared at Serena. "You have to be joking this time."

"Nope. I'm pretty sure I read or heard about it."

"But the real Mother Goose is buried there?"

"Well, her name was Elizabeth Vergoose, and she was nicknamed 'Mother Goose.' As the legend goes, she's supposed to be the author of all those nursery rhymes we learned as kids."

The girls launched into animated recitals of "Jack and Jill," "Little Boy Blue," and "Humpty Dumpty," laughing as they sang. As they started in on "Hickory, Dickory, Dock," two preschoolers standing nearby joined in, and they laughed all the more.

They followed the bricks beneath their feet, navigating their way among other sightseers along the crowded sidewalk. After only a couple of blocks, they reached the wrought iron fence and gate of the third oldest cemetery in Boston. Inside they found a plaque showing a map of the cemetery and its famous graves.

"See that?" said Serena, pointing to the plaque. "It says that Mother Goose is buried here, but no one is precisely sure where anymore." She looked back at the map. "Now if I can figure this out, we can find Paul Revere's grave as well as John Hancock's and Samuel Adams's. Serena stared at the paths shown on the plaque and then looked towards the grave markers, trying to decide which way to go.

Carly glanced at the map for a few seconds and then started off down a path towards the back of the cemetery. The girls strolled past the two-hundred-year-old graves and marveled at the old headstones, some sticking up from the ground at odd angles due to the settling of the ground as well as to the moving of some of the headstones for one reason or another over the centuries.

"There are skeletons on most of the grave markers," said Carly. She looked at some others. "And skulls, too. That is so creepy. Why would anyone want that on a gravestone? Flowers and stuff I can see, but bones?"

Serena shrugged. "Beats me. Maybe we should have hockey sticks engraved on our tombstones," she suggested.

Carly rolled her eyes at Serena.

"Oh, look," Serena continued, "there's Paul Revere's tombstone."

"Wow," said Carly, eyeing the tall statue from its base to its top. "What a monument. I wonder if I'll be remembered with such a huge statue?"

"Only if you warn the folks in Bar Harbor that the British are coming," answered Serena, giggling.

After viewing patriot Samuel Adams's grave and the markers of the victims of the Boston Massacre, Serena suggested they move on down the trail.

"I don't think my thieves are going to attempt grave robbing today," she said.

"Finally, some common sense," announced Carly.

Serena gazed across the cemetery to still another tall, stone grave marker. "I think that's John Hancock's memorial," said Serena, "patriotic comrade of Sam Adams. He's the one that

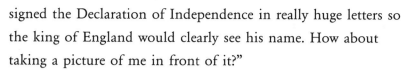

signed the Declaration of Independence in really huge letters so the king of England would clearly see his name. How about taking a picture of me in front of it?"

The girls walked over, and Serena positioned herself in front of the monument while Carly attached the proper lens to her camera. When she was ready, she told Serena to smile, but just as she was ready to shoot, she stopped.

"What's wrong?" asked Serena.

"Oh, the people standing on the other side of the marker are casting shadows onto the path in front of the stone. I don't like shadows in my pictures."

Serena curiously peeked around the side of the monument. When she saw a man and woman dressed in colonial clothes, she inhaled so suddenly that she made a funny squeaking noise, drawing the couple's attention to her.

The woman saw Carly with her camera and turned to Serena. "I guess we're ruining your picture, aren't we?" she asked.

The pair moved away from the tower, passing by Carly as they did. The man looked at Carly and stared for a second. "Bad sunburn," he said. "I get that way, too."

Carly smiled at him, then placed her camera up to her eye again. She jumped. Serena was directly in front of her, her eyes bugged out and wild.

"It's them!" she exclaimed.

CHAPTER TEN

Freedom Trail Chase

 Carly studied the man and woman as they walked down the path.

"Are you sure it's them?" she asked Serena. She got no answer. She turned and didn't see her anywhere. "Serena? Where are you?"

"Shhh," came a sound from behind the monument. "Wait until they leave the cemetery, and then we can start to follow them."

"Are you nuts?" she asked. "The man noticed my sunburn. He's bound to recognize me again."

"So we'll stay far enough behind him so he doesn't see us. C'mon."

Serena and Carly strolled a half block behind the colonial couple, blending in with the other tourists but always keeping their two suspects in view. They turned down School Street and passed the King's Chapel and the Old Corner Bookstore. Serena read the information in her book on both structures.

"What is that?" said Carly suddenly.

Serena looked up and saw a bright pink vehicle that looked

part army tank and part boat. "Boston Duck Tours" was printed in black along the sides with a number to call for information. "I think it's one of those amphibious landing vehicles."

"Amphibious landing vehicles?" questioned Carly, looking puzzled.

"Oh, you know," answered Serena. "They're those sea and land boats that were used during World War II. The Americans sailed in them off the big navy boats, and when they reached land, they rolled out of the water and right up onto the beaches. My dad has a model of one. These boats probably drive around Boston and then into the harbor as part of their tour."

Serena checked her costumed folks ahead and saw them turn left. When they reached the Old State House and Museum, Boston's oldest public building, the man and woman paused outside. The girls hung back a bit and tried to blend in with a tour group.

"Carly," said Serena. "Why don't you get a picture of them since they've stopped?" She handed the camera to her.

"Yuk!" exclaimed Carly as she retrieved her camera from inside its case. "What is all over my camera?" She examined the gooey, chocolate substance smeared on the side of the camera and, after smelling and touching it, hesitantly tasted it. "This is chocolate icing." She reached in further and pulled out a crumbled chocolate doughnut. "Yours, I presume?"

"Sorry," said Serena. "I was just being prepared for a hunger attack like you."

"Well, it's a good thing I came prepared with tissues," chided Carly as she wiped off her camera.

"Ohhh," said Serena in frustration. "The woman is leaving. You missed the shot."

"Well, it wasn't my fault," Carly protested, loudly.

"C'mon," said Serena. "Our man is entering the Old State House."

Inside the museum, a large room opened in front of them. Serena and Carly stood on tiptoes, searching for the three-cornered hat that was perched on the man's head.

"There he is," whispered Carly. She pointed discreetly across the room.

"Can you get a picture of him?"

Carly nodded. "I think so."

As Carly prepared her camera, Serena watched her suspected thief. First he casually walked past the artifact exhibits, glancing in the glass cases, acting like he wasn't really all that interested in them. Dozens of people lingered around a large display case in the center of the room, viewing the muskets and powder horns used during the Battle of Bunker Hill and loose tea from the Tea Party Ship. Paintings of important early Americans such as Paul Revere lined the walls, along with original letters and other valuable documents mounted in smaller, hanging display cases.

Serena watched the man ease up to one of the smaller cases. After studying the document inside, he examined how the wooden frame was fastened to the wall. Then he reached into his pocket, pulled out a small spiral notebook, and began writing in it. He even appeared to be drawing something.

Serena looked at one of the frames near her and was horrified when she saw it was fastened to the wall with ordinary screws. In his official-looking colonial disguise, the man could easily remove them with a small screwdriver and slip the contents out from behind the glass without causing suspicion.

Serena saw Carly moving in for her shot. After getting her attention, she motioned to her to take it right then so they'd have a picture of the man studying the artifact cases.

Carly aimed and snapped. They gave each other a thumbs-up at her success, but Serena quickly returned her attention back to her suspect, who had stopped at a case that held an old model of the USS *Constitution*. He carefully inspected it, and Serena could see a scowl form on his face. After checking the case out a few minutes later, she was relieved to find that the model would remain safe since the glass case was permanently sealed.

With his investigation completed, the man slipped out the door. Serena and Carly hurried out close behind him so they could see which way he went. But they needn't have worried; he was quickly striding over the bricks of the Freedom Trail in the same direction they had been heading before.

"I think I got a good picture of him," said Carly as they left the State House.

"Fantastic!" said Serena. "We need to get clear, close-up shots every time he does something suspicious so we'll have proof to give the police."

Carly studied her Freedom Trail map. "Well, it may be tough to stay as close to him as we need to. It looks like he's headed to Faneuil Hall and Quincy Market, where it's bound to be really crowded. I hope we don't lose him."

"That is not an option," Serena said, firmly. "We'll just have to stay on his tail but not so close that he notices us."

They crossed over the site of the Boston Massacre, marked by a star on the sidewalk encircled by cobblestones.

"Five people died here in 1770 when British soldiers opened fire on an angry mob protesting taxes," explained Serena to Carly as they stopped to read the engraved words. They continued following Colonial Man towards Faneuil Hall, an eighteenth-century market hall with a curious gold-plated grasshopper weathervane on its roof. Both girls craned their necks back to watch it spinning around and around in the breeze blowing in from the harbor. Suddenly Serena remembered what she should have been looking at and wrenched her neck down, frantically scanning the crowd for the colonial man.

"Where is he?" asked Serena, worry rising in her voice.

"I see him," said Carly a few seconds later. "He's over by that flower display."

"Let's go," said Serena.

The girls made their way through the bricked plaza between Faneuil Hall and Quincy Market and the two long buildings on either side of it, the North and South Markets, keeping Colonial Man in sight.

They passed a magician performing tricks, using tourists as his helpers. Nearby an artist sketched a portrait of a small boy who was beginning to wiggle, undoubtedly tired of having to sit still. Brightly colored balloons bounced in the air at a booth, fastened tightly to a pole until the vendor released one and handed it to a mother who tied it securely to her toddler's wrist.

The smell of barbecue wafted on the air, mingling with flower smells and other aromas that the girls couldn't identify. From the other end of the marketplace piano playing and singing blended in with the incredible hubbub coming from the hundreds of people gathered there for as many reasons as there were people.

"He's going inside," said Serena, suddenly.

Inside Faneuil Hall, the costumed man bought coffee and a paper and sat down at a small table.

"Good," said Carly. "He's taking a break. I'm tired and hungry."

"Me, too," agreed Serena. "But I guess my doughnut is history." She looked around at the wares of the food vendors inside. "Oooh," she said. "Jelly beans." She turned to Carly. "Keep an eye on him while I get some jelly beans."

"That sounds like a nourishing snack," commented Carly.

"Who's after nutrition?" she asked.

Serena eyed the bins of jelly beans that came in every color and in a myriad of flavors—bubble gum, chocolate mousse, grape jelly, buttered popcorn, even pickle. After choosing several different kinds, she dumped them all together in a paper bag that the clerk weighed.

"Want some jelly beans?" she asked Carly who was sitting on a step just outside the door.

Carly reached into the jelly bean bag and popped some into her mouth. A horrible look crossed her face as she chewed and swallowed. "That was awful! It tasted like peanut butter and pickles mixed with caramel corn and watermelon."

"It probably was," said Serena. "What's our guy doing?"

"He was just sipping coffee and reading the sports page a minute ago."

Serena peeked inside, looking towards the tables at the coffee booth. Her eyes widened, and her head jerked as she searched the tables and surrounding aisles for the man. "He's not there!" she exclaimed.

"What?" said Carly, jumping up. "I just checked on him."

"Then he can't have gotten far," said Serena. "You head down that way, and I'll check up here. If you don't find him, come back my way since I may have spotted him, and I'll do the same. We've got to keep looking until we find him!"

CHAPTER ELEVEN

Robbery at the Revere House

 Serena wove in and out of the crowds of tourists and Bostonians, surveying their clothes, looking for 1700s attire. She worked her way to the end of Faneuil Hall and was ready to return to Carly to see if she had spotted him, when suddenly she caught sight of a long, blue cape, dark knickers, knee-high stockings, and buckled shoes. When the crowd thinned in front of her, she saw the three-cornered hat.

Serena quickly trailed her man across the cobblestones and bricks into Quincy Market. She lurked behind some kids buying sandwiches and saw him get in line at one of the food booths. After purchasing soup and a sandwich, he worked his way towards the eating area. All the tables downstairs were full, so he marched up the steps to an additional seating area. Serena followed, wondering how Carly would ever find her.

The suspect was blowing on a spoonful of soup when someone nudged Serena. It was Carly. "How did you find me?" Serena asked. Then her forehead wrinkled. "And why are you wearing a Red Sox cap?"

"So he won't recognize me so easily," Carly answered, as she slung her camera bag over Serena's shoulder. "Anyway, I didn't see him anywhere on my end, so I started hiking back towards you. On the way it occurred to me that what I was carrying seemed heavier. I discovered you took off without my camera."

"Sorry," said Serena.

"Well, I'll forgive you this time, because I suddenly realized that if I put on my telephoto lens, I'd be able to see things in the distance. When I looked through the camera, I saw you following him into Quincy Market. I didn't see you anywhere on the first floor, so I came up here."

The girls silently observed their prey taking a bite out of his sandwich.

"It's gonna take a while for him to eat all that," said Serena. "Maybe we should grab some lunch, too. We don't know when we might get another chance."

Carly agreed and decided to get them each a bowl of clam chowder, another Boston specialty, and a soda from the nearest food booth. Serena found a table close enough to Colonial Man to see what he was doing but not so close that he might recognize them. While she waited, she read through the historical notes in her guidebook about the rest of the sites they would come to on the trail.

When Carly returned, the girls eagerly spooned their creamy soup. Suddenly, Serena choked on a mouthful as another man approached their costumed gentleman and sat down with him, his back towards the girls. The men leaned towards each other, talking intently. The girls watched as their suspect pulled out his notebook and handed it to the other man.

"That man must be part of the smuggling ring," spluttered Serena, still feeling the effects of the hot soup in her windpipe. "The costumed man is showing him whatever he wrote or drew in the notebook when he was in the Old State House. Maybe the colonial guy works for him." She paused. "In fact, I think I've seen him somewhere."

"You can't be sure this guy is involved or even of what's in Colonial Man's notebook," countered Carly.

"But I am sure," said Serena. "The two of them are connected somehow as well as the colonial woman he was with this morning."

"Maybe they're just guides, employed by the city, and he was making sure that the displays were safe," suggested Carly.

Serena thought for a minute, going back through all she'd learned the past week. "We saw this man and the colonial woman at Paul Revere's house," she began. "I have pictures that show the missing candle mold. The news reported that first tea and now a duckling are missing. We've seen the man with the woman again today, lurking in the shadows of the cemetery. And in the Old State House, he inspected the display cases holding valuable artifacts, making diagrams and whispering into a tape recorder. We've followed him along the Freedom Trail, and now we've caught him discussing his findings with this other man." Serena inhaled. "I know it's all connected somehow."

"I still think your imagination is working overtime," said Carly, "but why don't I get a picture of him with this other guy anyway."

"Great idea," Serena said.

Carly moved into position behind a large decorative plant along one wall. She aimed and shot. She took another from a slightly different angle, trying to capture more of his face. When she took the third shot, the colonial man's head snapped up and angrily scanned the room. He said something to the other man and he, too, began looking around. Carly pulled her hat down to cover her face and eased her camera to the floor by the strap so they couldn't identify who'd been snapping pictures.

"That was close," said Carly, returning to Serena.

"Yeah, a little bit," she agreed. "But it looks like you got some good pictures of their faces."

"Let's hope so," she answered.

"Uh-oh," said Serena. "Our men are leaving."

They followed them outside. While the recent arrival turned and walked briskly across the courtyard, Colonial Man turned towards the street. Back on the sidewalk, he picked up the Freedom Trail and continued north.

"I'll bet he's headed back to Paul Revere's house," Serena said.

"Why?" questioned Carly. "According to you, he's already made his heist there."

"Yeah, and he got away with it. Maybe he figures to strike again."

The duo trailed him from a distance down narrow bricked streets flanked by brick sidewalks. The roads twisted this way and that, joined from time to time by alleys intersecting at sharp angles. Some of the passageways, originally designed to be only wide enough for carriages to rumble through, were barely large enough for a car.

"Strawberries!" yelled a voice. "Fresh and juicy."

"Get your melons here. Fresh vegetables. Cucumbers," called another.

"What is this place?" asked Carly as they entered a blocked-off street filled with table upon table of food. "Some funky outside grocery store?"

"It's the Haymarket," Serena answered. "It's open on Fridays and Saturdays, and vendors sell all kinds of produce."

The girls squeezed through the aisles of pushcarts, turning down the sales pitches of the vendors hawking their produce. Music blared from loudspeakers, and when mixed with the shouting, made it impossible for the girls to hear each other without almost screaming. Serena and Carly inched past locals and tourists alike waiting in line behind wooden platforms displaying neat rows of oranges, eggplants, honeydew melons, cantaloupes, bananas, celery, potatoes, cabbage, tomatoes, corn, and grapes.

Colonial Man wasn't interested in produce either and quickly made his way past the market and into a tunnel that led underneath the highway.

"Are you sure we're still on the Freedom Trail?" asked Serena.

"The sign up there says so," Carly answered, pointing. "I think this tunnel just goes under all the construction they're doing through the old part of the city to allow traffic to flow more easily. Claire told me it's called the 'big dig' or something like that. It's been under construction for years."

They looked down into an enormous hole with backhoes and bulldozers sitting on the bottom.

"It looks like they still have a long way to go," mused Serena at the dug-up and nowhere-near-done construction site.

After emerging from the tunnel, they walked a few more blocks, and the oldest part of Boston, the original town, opened up before them.

"I feel like I just entered Italy," said Carly, observing the many Italian restaurants stuck in among neat, brick row homes. Some of the houses and restaurants had the flag of Italy displayed in front. Though there were no yards and few trees, many houses' window ledges had flower boxes attached to them and were ablaze with brightly colored geraniums and petunias and trailing vines.

"The North End is mostly Italian now," said Serena.

"What's that bunch of people doing up there?" Carly asked, noticing a group of people gathering and the crowd growing larger.

"I read in my book that in August the Italian neighborhood holds several festivals to honor different patron saints in the Catholic Church. They must be gearing up for one now."

As they approached Paul Revere's homestead, they slowed, all at once wondering how they would follow the man into the house with so many tourists waiting to tour it.

"And we can't take pictures," Carly reminded Serena.

"We'll just have to be eyewitnesses then," said Serena, as she paid for her ticket and entered the herb garden.

They mingled with other visitors in the far corner of the brick courtyard, keeping an eye on the man in costume. Suddenly, Serena inhaled sharply.

"What is it?" Carly asked.

"The colonial woman just came down the back stairs of the house."

The girls watched the woman greet their man near the door.

"C'mon," said Serena. "We need to get closer. See if you can get a picture."

They wriggled their way to the door and eased in among the group waiting to go into the house next, trying to act like they belonged in the group and had stepped away briefly and now had returned to claim their spots. Carly fiddled with her camera and managed to get a shot of the two conversing. So many other cameras were whirring and flashing around them that the two guides didn't notice Carly's camera aimed directly at them.

The costumed woman opened the door to let in the next group of people. The man slid in past her, looking like he was part of the tour. Serena and Carly tried to force their way towards the door as politely as they could, fearing that the door would close before they got in. The people in front of them entered one at a time into the kitchen.

Serena watched the woman, her head bobbing and her lips forming numbers as each person entered. The girls inched closer. Just as Serena put her foot on the threshold, the woman reached over and closed the door.

"That's all I can allow in for now," she said to the folks lined up. "But it will only be a five-minute wait, and then I can let you in to begin your tour."

The two waited for what seemed like five hours rather than five minutes, both staring at the ground, fearing the woman would recognize them. Finally, she opened the door and stepped into the room. The girls and the group behind them followed her in. Other tourists were exiting the kitchen, but up near the hearth stood the colonial man, acting like he was one of the guides on duty.

Serena and Carly were pushed towards the hearth by the throng of people coming in after them. Carly pulled her cap down over her eyes, and Serena buried her face in her tour book. Every few seconds she glanced up and viewed the man, never moving her head from its downward position.

Serena stretched from side to side around the other people, trying to see the spot where the candle mold was—is! Serena gawked. There sat the mold on the floor, right next to the popcorn popper! But her pictures showed an empty space there.

A wave of doubt washed over her. Maybe the mold had just been moved temporarily.

But as Serena moved in for a closer look, she suddenly realized the tin looked far too shiny to be a hundred or more years old. She remembered Mr. Cantwell showing her some of his tin antiques—a cup and some plates—and how the metal had darkened and dulled with age. This one looked like someone had scratched it up a bit to eliminate that new, shiny look.

Serena worked her way back through the crowd and stood next to Carly. She whispered to her, and then Carly looked at the candle mold. Serena continued watching the man, waiting for him to make a move, which she hoped would be soon since people were exiting the kitchen and moving into the sitting room next door.

Not knowing what else to do, the girls followed the others towards the adjoining room. As they neared the door, the colonial man moved over to the huge hutch along the wall and pulled out from behind it a heavy-duty canvas shopping bag with handles.

The woman glanced at him, concern on her face, as he struggled to lift the bag and its obviously-very-heavy-something inside. Serena stood on tiptoes to try to see the contents of the bag. The man clasped it closed suddenly and brushed past the girls and into the sitting room, but not before Serena caught a glimpse of something shiny.

CHAPTER TWELVE

After That Duck!

 Serena turned to Carly, speechless. She pushed her through the doorway and into a corner of the sitting room and began to whisper. "Did you see what was in the bag?"

"No," answered Carly. "I was too far back."

"I swear I saw a glint of bronze. And judging by how he struggled with lifting the bag, I'm pretty sure about what was inside."

"The duck?"

"The duck."

"What now?" asked Carly.

"We keep following him and see what he does with it," Serena answered.

The girls followed Colonial Man up the stairs into the bedroom. A couple dozen sightseers mingled about, admiring the colonial period furniture as well as the diamond-shaped panes of purplish glass in the windows.

They spied their thief in the corner next to the locked glass display case. The bag sat on the floor between his legs. One of

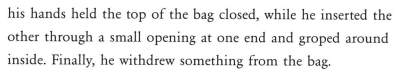

his hands held the top of the bag closed, while he inserted the other through a small opening at one end and groped around inside. Finally, he withdrew something from the bag.

"Excuse me," he said to the visitors gathered near the case. The people moved away while Colonial Man inserted a key in the lock and opened the case. "I just need to take out some of the artifacts," he said to those nearby, "for some historians to study."

Serena's eyes opened wide as she heard the thief's explanation, realizing just how easy it was for him to steal something right out in the open. She remembered that during her previous visit, in which she had carefully studied every artifact, the case had been filled with original writings about Paul Revere as well as other artifacts. She watched in horror as Colonial Man slid some objects into his bag through an opening just big enough for them. Then he rearranged the remaining items in the case and relocked it with the key.

As he moved towards the back steps, Serena and Carly worked their way to the display case. Serena stared intently at the items in the case, recalling the artifacts she had viewed so excitedly the week before.

"I'm positive an original copy of a book with Henry Wadsworth Longfellow's poem 'Paul Revere's Ride' is missing," said Serena. "And a letter of Paul Revere's is gone, too." She studied the shelves some more. "I know there was something else in the front," she said, "but I can't remember what."

"What an ingenious way to steal stuff," said Carly.

 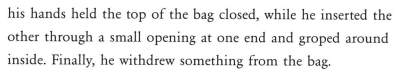

"So you finally believe me?" asked Serena.

"Yeah," Carly nodded. "It does appear that he took something from the display case. I wish I could have captured him on film."

Serena and Carly quickly walked through the back bedroom and down the steps to the courtyard.

"Why's he hanging by the door?" wondered Carly when they'd spotted him.

Suddenly the door opened, and Colonial Woman appeared and began welcoming and counting the next tour group. As their robber eased up next to her, Carly grabbed her camera. Just as he handed the woman something, Carly's camera buzzed. Then Colonial Man turned abruptly and strode through the herb garden and back to the street.

"I caught him passing the key back to her," exclaimed Carly triumphantly.

"The key? Are you sure?"

Carly smiled. "Saw it through my telephoto lens."

"Great," said Serena. They did high fives, the other tourists in the courtyard eyeing them strangely.

"Let's go," said Serena, "before he gets too far ahead."

As the girls followed Colonial Man across the cobblestoned street, Serena tripped over the uneven stones imbedded in the road and almost fell. They continued on the Freedom Trail for a couple of blocks, which led them into a long, brick courtyard and past an enormous statue of Paul Revere on a horse, depicting him riding through the countryside calling his compatriots "to arms."

"Now that statue is definitely safe," commented Serena, looking up at it rising high above her head.

As the girls neared the end of the courtyard, the Old North Church loomed in front of them. They followed their man inside. Carly checked on her camera.

"I don't see a sign that says I can't take pictures anywhere," she said.

"Me neither," agreed Serena. "So be prepared."

They saw the thief slip into box pew number fifty-four, the Revere family box, at the rear of the church and next to a window. The girls quickly slid into box pew number forty-four, two boxes back and on the other side of the aisle. A column was located in the corner of their box, providing them with something to hide behind while enjoying the good view they had of their suspect. In the front of the church a costumed guide was explaining the history of the church to the crowds of people who continually filtered in and out of the building.

"The eight bells in the church belfry range in weight from 620 pounds to 1,545 pounds," said the guide. "Fifteen-year-old Paul Revere and some friends provided regular bell ringing and were on call for other occasions like sounding an alarm."

"I didn't know that," muttered Serena.

"Amazing," laughed Carly. "There's actually something in our history that you didn't know."

The guide continued her spiel, telling the role the Old North Church played in the revolutionaries' battle for freedom. They listened to the familiar story of the lanterns in the steeple, signaling to Paul Revere the British soldiers' movement by sea.

"Why are we sitting inside a box?" whispered Carly, studying the four chest-high sides rising around her. Inside the box were two wooden benches. Across the front Bibles and hymnals were neatly arranged in a wooden holder.

"To keep the heat in," answered Serena. "Colonial churches didn't have any source of heat." She pointed to tin boxes with holes punched in them sitting on the windowsills next to some of the boxes. "Those are foot warmers," she said. "The people filled them with hot coals from their fires at home and brought them to church and put them on the floor of their pew box. Mr. Cantwell has an old bed warmer that was used the same way except it was for warming the bed. He said it's one of his most valuable antiques since it's so old and rare."

Serena watched Carly lean first to one side of the pillar and then to the other. "What are you doing?" she asked.

"Oh, no," Carly groaned.

"What is it?" asked Serena.

"Look at the windowsill along our man's box."

"There's nothing there," said Serena, as she scanned the wide, wooden ledge. "But I gather from your reaction that there was a foot warmer there a few minutes ago?"

Carly nodded. "I wish I'd had my camera ready."

"Well, get a picture of the empty sill. I'm sure somebody official can verify that there was a warmer in that box."

They waited until the smuggler left his pew, and then Carly shot pictures of that ledge as well as all the other windowsills in the church. Then they headed out of the church to catch up with their prey.

The girls watched him lug his heavy bag, leaning to the left to counterbalance the weight in his right hand. Every so often he switched hands. A couple of times he put the bag down to rest his arms.

Serena laughed. "Next time he should pick lighter artifacts to steal."

"Where do you suppose he's taking all this stuff?" asked Carly.

"I have no idea," answered Serena. "But he certainly isn't going to lug these things any farther than he has to."

After walking a few more blocks, they approached Copp's Hill Burying Ground. "Legend has it," said Serena, "that grave robbers once stole two bodies and carved their own names into the markers so they could be used for their own burials." She pointed across the street. "That's the narrowest house in Boston. People called them ten-footers when they were built, in the 1700s."

"Will you please stop giving me a history lesson?" exclaimed Carly. "I've heard enough about the sites of the Freedom Trail. Have you by any chance realized that we're almost to the end of the trail? Once we cross the Charlestown River, the only places left are the Charlestown Naval Yard and Bunker Hill. What do we do if he keeps going? I mean, it's—" she looked at her watch, "almost two o'clock. We have to be back at the Common by five."

"We can always ride the subway back," suggested Serena.

"Suppose he takes a bus or a taxi somewhere?"

Serena sighed. She really hadn't thought about any of these possibilities. "Then I guess we'll go back, get your pictures developed somewhere, show them to the police and hope they'll believe our story."

The girls walked in silence for a while. An ambulance raced down the street, its siren blaring and its lights flashing. Across the street, a man with a jackhammer bore into the street below, and a jet roared through the sky. If the girls had felt like talking, they wouldn't have heard each other anyway.

Soon they reached the Charlestown Bridge, which spans the Charles River. Halfway over the bridge, their thief stopped to rest. The girls quickly gazed out over the river, shielding their eyes from the sun and their faces from him. They hoped if he turned around and saw them he would think they were tourists admiring the view and not his trackers.

In a little while he continued on across the bridge, but he stumbled from the duck's weight and fell over backwards, landing right on his rear end. Serena covered her mouth to stifle her laughter as the thief jumped up and continued walking as though nothing had happened.

A short distance ahead, Colonial Man veered off to the right and into a large open area along the Charles River—the Charlestown Navy Yard. Carly and Serena followed Colonial Man, hugging the shadows of several old brick buildings located along the wide walkway. Off to their right were several wharfs jutting out into the water, one of which was home to Boston's most famous ship, the USS *Constitution*. In a grassy area on the opposite side of the walkway from the wharfs, two drummers and two fife players in period clothes warmed up to play. Carly and Serena joined the other visitors gathering to hear them. As they began "Yankee Doodle," Serena spied their suspect walking up the gangplank of the *Constitution*.

"Get your telephoto lens on your camera," said Serena. "We've got to see what he's going to do next."

CHAPTER THIRTEEN

Hiding Out

 Carly peered through her telephoto lens and saw Colonial Man board the *Constitution*. She reported to Serena that he nodded at one of the guides on the boat, dressed up as a sailor, who nodded back. Then he moved to the end of the boat and out of Carly's view.

Serena couldn't stand not being able to see him. She insisted they had to get on the boat to see if he intended to pass off something from the bag or steal something else.

"What's he going to steal off the boat?" asked Carly. "A cannonball or something?"

"Probably not," said Serena, "although a real cannonball that landed on 'Old Ironsides' would be quite a valuable artifact."

"Old Ironsides?" asked Carly, raising a questioning eyebrow at her.

Serena looked at her and shook her head. "You are hopeless. The boat was nicknamed 'Old Ironsides' because cannonballs bounced off her heavy wooden hull as if it were made of iron. Anyway," she continued, "we need to get on the boat. We can't tell what he's doing from out here."

At that moment, a tour bus pulled up to the curb. It was filled with senior citizens, women mostly, who stiffly and carefully stepped off the bus and grouped together on the sidewalk. As their tour guide led them towards the *Constitution*, Serena nudged Carly to fall in line behind them, suggesting they could blend in with the group as it boarded.

"Right," said Carly. "They all have white hair and white skin, are over seventy, and are dressed in polyester pantsuits." She stood back and slowly surveyed the opposite picture they presented.

"So we'll just use them as cover. Several of them are heavy enough to hide behind."

Serena chose a large woman in a lavender skirt with matching jacket and traipsed behind her. Carly found a man holding his wife's arm as they walked, the two of them adequately providing her with something to hide behind in the event Colonial Man looked her way.

When the girls reached the deck they scanned the tourists, searching for the colonial clothes that would stand out among them. They discovered him standing at the side, staring out to sea. Serena and Carly positioned themselves where they could see him in case he made a move.

Serena took a moment to stare at the huge masts rising above her head, the ropes and rigging running every which way, reminding her of a spider's web. Cannons sat at openings on the sides of the deck, just as they had many years before, when they hurled cannonballs at enemy ships. She tried to picture the boat underway on the open seas, its huge sails unfurled to catch the ocean breezes.

She turned her attention then to a guide, who was dressed as an 1812 sailor and was talking about the *Constitution*'s stellar history as a battleship. "Who knows what nickname she was given during the War of 1812?" he asked. All the folks from the tour group called out "Old Ironsides."

"See," said Serena. "They all know their history."

"They were probably alive when it happened," Carly countered.

"They'd be over two hundred years old."

"Some of them look that old."

"You're just jealous that they knew the answer."

"How many of them could surf the Internet?" Carly asked.

"Touché," said Serena.

After the tour ended, they hovered near the exit, watching their man. He casually slid up to another costumed guide and opened the bag. The man glanced in and then pointed to the museum next door.

Serena and Carly raced across the parking lot and entered the museum building. They ducked into the gift shop and wove their way through the store, picking a tall book display to hide behind as they watched the lobby through the door for their thief, hoping he would enter the gift shop and not the museum. But if he did pick the museum, the girls would pay for admission so they could continue to follow him.

While they waited, Serena noticed a sign near the door that said that photography was not allowed in the building. She elbowed Carly and pointed to the sign.

"What is it with no picture taking everywhere?" Carly asked.

"I think it has something to do with ownership of artifacts and copyrights on . . ." said Serena, her voice trailing off. "He just walked in," she whispered. They watched Colonial Man survey the shoppers in the store, all busy with finding the right souvenir or gift to take home. He then moved over to the large checkout counter in the front corner of the store, where several clerks waited on customers. Colonial Man glanced at one of them, who was dressed in an 1812 sailor's uniform.

The girls, from their vantage point behind the book rack and shelves lined with boat models, had a perfect view of the counter. They peered through the small space between the shelves while remaining completely hidden themselves.

"Can you take a picture without your flash?" Serena asked Carly.

"Yeah, but it'll be too dark, and you probably won't be able to see anything. Besides, I'm not going to risk being seen with a camera held up to my face."

"Just let it hang around your neck then. It should be at the right height to get a picture. When our guy does something, just casually reach up and push the button, like you accidentally bumped it or something."

"Are you going to bail me out of jail after they haul me away for breaking their rules?"

"Don't be ridiculous," said Serena. "Get ready," she hissed suddenly.

Carly positioned herself in front of the few-inches-wide gap between the displays and adjusted her lens to what she thought would be the right distance for capturing the shot. When the clerk finished with his customer, Colonial Man brazenly walked behind the counter and handed over his bag to the clerk. Carly inched her hand up to scratch her elbow and pushed the button on her camera as she did.

The two costumed men bent over the bag for a few seconds. Then Colonial Man picked it up again, and the clerk handed him a bulging white envelope. After checking the tourists in the shop to make sure no one was paying attention to them, Colonial Man abruptly left the store.

The girls waited a few minutes for Colonial Man to exit the building and then they left the gift shop. Just as they rounded the corner of the building outside, they froze. There sat Colonial Man on a bench, his back to them, counting a wad of money in the envelope he'd just received from the clerk.

The girls backed up a bit, and Carly adjusted her camera lens. While a family posed for pictures nearby, Carly snapped a photo of Colonial Man counting the money. When he'd finished, he started strolling back through the navy yard, walking perfectly upright and swinging his bag at his side.

"He doesn't seem to be having trouble carrying his bag anymore," Carly said, grinning at Serena.

Serena laughed out loud. "I think our duck flew the coop!"

"Can we quit now," asked Carly, "since we've got proof that he's selling these things for money?"

Serena shook her head. "Your pictures might not show anything without the flash," she said. "Besides, he's heading towards Bunker Hill. We need to see what he does there."

"At least we have to end there," announced Carly. "That's the last stop on the Freedom Trail."

Serena said nothing. She knew that was the end of the trail, but it might not be the end to her investigation. If her suspect continued, so would she.

They followed him through Charlestown's quaint streets lined with homes dating from Boston's earliest days, and soon reached the two square blocks of the Bunker Hill Monument, part of the Boston National Historic Park.

"It's actually Breed's Hill," Serena said, "but the Boston soldiers built an earthen bunker here against the advance of British soldiers."

Carly shot Serena an exasperated look.

"Sorry," Serena said. "I'll shut up."

The girls stared upwards at the granite monument rising high into the air. Out of the corner of her eye, though, Serena saw Colonial Man enter the tower. The girls hurried after him. When they reached the door to the tower, they stopped, knowing they couldn't risk meeting up with him at the top or on the steps.

A few feet away was another park building. The girls went in and found battle displays, re-created with toy-sized soldiers, cannons, and horses situated on a large topographical display table in the main lobby area. Although Serena didn't know if anything there was of historical value, she was still relieved the entire display was enclosed in glass for its preservation and protection from tourists—and thieves. And with a park ranger standing nearby answering folks' questions, Serena felt an added sense of protection.

Serena and Carly rested on a bench in the lobby with a view of the door to the tower. Suddenly they saw Colonial Man, heading right towards them. The girls looked away just as he veered right and into the hallway where the rest rooms were.

"Let's get out of here," said Serena.

"Gladly," Carly answered.

They hid on the side of the building, waiting for him to exit. When he did, the girls stared at him, now realizing that he no longer carried a bag; instead, he had a backpack slung over a shoulder.

"He must have passed off the bag at the top of the tower," said Serena, "to someone waiting for him up there."

"Who?" asked Carly.

"How would I know?" she asked. "But it doesn't look like he's got the foot warmer anymore. The bag looks too flat. Let's keep tracking him, and maybe we'll get some answers."

They followed him down several streets, staying a block behind him and out of view. Carly searched the Boston map and told Serena that a T station was not too far ahead and suggested he was planning to board there. She was right. They waited until he'd disappeared down the steps, and then they entered the subway.

It wasn't nearly as crowded at this stop on the underground transit as the ones closer to the busy business district. A train approached on the opposite tracks heading north and out of the city. Within a few minutes, though, the bright light of a T filled the tunnel in front of them. Colonial Man and the girls entered the train by different doors and sped away into the dark.

After the train stopped at North Station and then Haymarket, Colonial Man began to gather up his backpack. Serena poked Carly and told her to be ready to jump. After exiting the train, they trailed their suspect up the orange hallway and turned down a blue one. They passed the man with the saxophone they'd seen the week before. Serena dug in her pocket and deposited some change into his open case.

They boarded a train when Colonial Man did, but once again they found themselves with no place to sit. But they didn't have to stand for long. At the very next stop, he got off the train, and they followed him onto the street.

"Where are we?" asked Serena.

"Well, this is the subway stop for the New England Aquarium," said Carly, pointing. "It's that building over there."

"Great," Serena said. "I suppose now he's going to steal some fish!"

CHAPTER FOURTEEN

Discovered

Serena and Carly studied the jagged points of the building's exterior as they got closer. The odd angles of walls and freestanding sculpture reminded them of the rocky coastline back home. The walls, covered with stainless-steel panels, created a shimmering effect similar to that of the scales on a fish.

Outside the aquarium was an enormous water tank built into the side of the building. Gliding through the water were seals, swimming and rolling after each other, entertaining the visitors as they waited in line to buy tickets. Serena watched the spotted swimmers, with their large eyes and whiskered cheeks, just on the other side of the glass, wishing she could stay and watch. But she had more important business to attend to. She got in line for a ticket and motioned for Carly to line up with her.

"Oh, Serena," Carly fussed. "I don't want to buy another ticket for something I don't want to see. This investigation of yours is beginning to get expensive." She checked the money in her wallet. "I'm getting low."

"Yeah, me too," said Serena as she realized her money had dwindled as the day wore on with the admission fees they'd paid at several places. She looked at Carly. "I promise I'll pay you back. But we have to keep following Colonial Man. I doubt there's anything of historical value here, so maybe he's going to turn over the rest of the artifacts to someone. If you can get pictures of that, then we should have enough evidence."

"Unless you can't take pictures in here either," grumbled Carly. "Maybe the fish are copyrighted."

"Just come on," she said. "He's already inside."

After paying for their tickets, they entered the aquarium lobby, keeping Colonial Man in sight but themselves out of his sight. They followed him into the main exhibition area and the most gigantic fish tank the girls had ever seen. Rising four stories high and containing two hundred thousand gallons of water, the tank was home to sharks, sea turtles, moray eels, and tropical fish of all sizes, shapes, and colors.

"I'd hate to have to clean out that fish tank," said Serena.

"The tropical fish are pretty cool," said Carly. "Look at the yellow striped ones over there and the blue and green ones. They sort of glow."

Serena looked at the fish Carly pointed out as well as others. She saw some with delicate tails that spread out and waved like a fan. Others were spotted or striped with contrasting colors. "My mom always says she misses the tropical fish she grew up seeing in the waters off the Philippines. She used to go snorkeling and says you could swim right along with the fish, just like you were one of them."

"Didn't she worry about sharks?" asked Carly. "I mean, look at those teeth."

Serena stepped back from the glass as a shark, its rows of sharp, triangular teeth gleaming in a nasty smile, swam slowly past her. "I don't know," Serena answered. "But I think I'd worry some."

They turned their attention to the turtles and eels as they waited for their man to move. Finally, they saw him motion to a man in a gray uniform pulling a trash bag out of a can.

"That guy looks like a janitor or something," said Carly.

"Maintenance man or biologist, just get a picture of him with our guy," instructed Serena.

The two men met by a door and talked for a few minutes. The janitor kept looking around, checking to see if anyone was watching. Carly and Serena eased their way around the fish tank and part way down the ramp to give Carly a better angle for a shot. The janitor opened the bag of trash he was holding, and Colonial Man unzipped the backpack. Carly snapped. The man lifted some papers and a book out of the backpack, and Carly shot again.

"That's the stuff from the case in Paul Revere's house!" exclaimed Serena.

Carly remained silent while she focused on her next shot. The janitor took the items and placed them in the trash bag. The camera buzzed again. Then the janitor reached into his back pocket and pulled out a brown envelope. Carly snapped a picture as he handed it to their suspect.

Suddenly, Colonial Man's head jerked directly towards the source of the camera flashes. His face scrunched into an ugly frown as he spied Carly with the camera. Serena saw his face and cringed as he stared at Carly, sure that he was wondering who she was and why she was taking pictures of him.

As Carly frantically put her camera into its case, she bumped her Red Sox cap and it fell to the floor, exposing her sunburned face in all its red glory. Serena groaned as she saw the look of recognition cross Colonial Man's face, guessing that he was recalling his encounter with Carly at the cemetery.

Carly scooped up her hat and turned to Serena. "He saw me!" she squeaked.

"I know," said Serena, already moving through the crowd. "I think he recognized you from this morning, too."

Carly's eyes bugged out.

"Don't panic," said Serena. "We'll lose him in the crowd." She darted one way and then the other, dodging kids and strollers, Carly trailing behind her. Serena grabbed Carly's hand and led her through the crowd towards an exhibit entitled "The Edge of the Sea." They tried to blend in with the folks gathered at the hands-on tidal pool where a biologist talked about starfish and placed real ones into the outstretched hands of several children.

"Do you see them anywhere?" Serena asked Carly.

"I'm too scared to look," she answered.

Serena surveyed the other fish, bird, and mammal exhibits around them. Not seeing the duo anywhere, they made a dash for the gift shop and hid behind a bin filled with stuffed sharks, birds, and fish of assorted colors and sizes. Serena sneaked a peek from behind the head of a multi-striped fish. "I don't see them anywhere. I think we lost Colonial Man back at the tidal pool exhibit. And I haven't seen the janitor since he handed over the envelope of money."

"Can we please get out of here then?" pleaded Carly.

Serena eyed the door and scanned the lobby. "Okay," she said. "Run!"

The girls galloped through the gift shop entrance, across the lobby, and out the doors. They kept running down the walk and crossed the street, barely even watching for traffic. After thundering noisily down the steps to the subway, the girls finally caught their breath.

"I think we did it!" announced Serena triumphantly. "I'll bet he's still looking for us back in the aquarium. All we have to do now is get your film to a photo shop."

"I'm not even going to argue with you," said Carly. "But I would like to know where this photo shop is."

Serena frowned. "I think I saw a drugstore this morning not too far from the Old South Meeting House. We can get it developed there."

Carly pulled out her subway map. "Then we need to get to State Street," she said, her voice rising over the sound of the incoming train.

They hopped on and rode to the next stop. When they returned to the street, they found themselves in the busy downtown shopping area filled with tourists and Bostonians alike. They were also right next door to the Old South Meeting House. After locating a drugstore a couple of doors down, they entered and found the photo-processing desk inside.

"The sign says 'in by ten a.m., pick up by five p.m. the same day,'" read Serena. She turned to Carly. "What time is it?"

"Well, it's obviously after ten," she replied.

"Then I guess we'll have to pick the film up tomorrow. Do you think your mom will mind making a quick stop here and then at the police station before we head home?"

"Are you kidding? When my mom hears about the stolen artifacts, sees the pictures, and joins forces with you, I'll be lucky if she wants to go home at all."

Serena smiled, but her smile quickly disappeared. "Uh-oh," she said, as she read another sign. "It says there's no service on weekends. We won't be able to get the rolls developed at all, at least not until Monday. We'll have to find another photo shop."

She asked the cashier and rolled her eyes when she was told there was a one-hour photo shop located just on the other side of the meetinghouse.

"We could have gone there in the first place," said Serena.

They traipsed out the door and retraced their steps towards the other store, neither noticing a man in a colonial costume lurking in the shadows across the street.

CHAPTER FIFTEEN

Trapped

The girls easily found the one-hour photo shop just past the Old South Meeting House, which capitalized on the tourists walking the Freedom Trail. They could drop off film, have lunch, or tour a historical site or two and then return to get their pictures. They could also enlarge a special shot and choose a frame for it, enabling them to display a remembrance of their Boston vacation as soon as they arrived home.

"How on earth did we miss this place before?" Serena asked.

"We were busy looking at one of the duck boats, I think, and must have walked right by," explained Carly as they entered the store.

"How long does it take to get a roll of film developed?" Serena asked the clerk behind the counter.

"We guarantee your pictures will be ready in less than an hour," she answered.

"That's great," said Serena as she laid the film on the counter.

"Except that the developing machine wasn't operating properly this morning so we're backed up with film to process."

"Backed up how far?" asked Serena.

"About two hours or so."

Serena smacked her palm on her head. "I do not believe this."

"I'm very sorry for the inconvenience," said the clerk, "but if you do wish to leave your film, we won't charge you for it." She pointed to a sign stating the store's guarantee: one-hour developing or the processing would be free.

"The price is right," suggested Carly.

"I agree," Serena said. She filled out the information on the processing bag and left it with the clerk. As they turned to leave, Serena did a double take as she glanced out the big front window towards the street. She stopped abruptly, and Carly smacked into her back.

"Why'd you stop?" she asked.

"Oh . . . no reason," Serena answered. But as they stepped onto the sidewalk, Serena quickly looked up and down the street. Seeing nothing, she shrugged and followed Carly. She was glad she hadn't voiced her feeling that she thought she saw someone in a colonial costume on the sidewalk, needlessly causing Carly to panic.

"So what do we do for the next two hours?" asked Carly.

"I have no idea," said Serena.

"Well, I do," Carly answered. "We can go tour the Children's Museum."

"Where's that?"

"Near the Tea Party Ship. I saw the sign last Saturday when we were there."

"What are we going to do at a museum for little kids?"

"It's not just for little kids. I looked at a brochure at the information center, and it has all kinds of cool things to do. There's also 'Teen Tokyo,' an exhibit about how teens live in Japan. Besides, there's nothing else to do for two hours, and you owe me for coming along on this ridiculous hunt of yours."

Serena thought for a minute. "Well then, if I go with you now, will you let me off the hook with shopping for clothes?"

"Deal," said Carly. "You're never much fun to shop with anyway."

"Lead the way," said Serena.

They headed to the T station and rode the Orange Line and then the Red Line to South Station. Carly led Serena down several streets until they reached the tea ship. As they walked past, they watched the current group of visitors toss boxes of tea into the water.

They crossed Fort Point Channel towards an old brick building with a banner hanging on the outside announcing the Children's Museum. But Serena and Carly's attention was focused on the large structure that stood between them and the entrance to the museum.

It appeared to be a food stand, and dozens of people were either waiting in line or milling about eating ice cream or sipping drinks. Others were taking pictures of the food stand.

"I don't believe what I'm seeing," said Serena.

"Why not? Haven't you ever seen a food stand in the shape of a milk bottle before?" Carly quizzed.

"Touché," Serena replied.

The girls stared at the huge bottle-building, rising four stories into the air and narrowing at the top just like an old-fashioned bottle. Its base, where the food was prepared, was about fifteen feet in diameter and had several windows for order taking and food pick-up.

"I'm getting ice cream when we leave," announced Carly.

"What's wrong with right now?" asked Serena.

They lined up at a window in the milk bottle behind several other customers. Serena ordered a root beer float and Carly a double fudge cone.

"This is heavenly," said Serena as she scooped a mound of vanilla ice cream from deep inside the cup filled with foamy root beer.

"Umm, hmm," mumbled Carly, deeply involved with her cone.

They sat on a bench, watching the tourists and some boats sail by on the river and enjoying their treats. When they finished, they walked to a trash can nearby to deposit their cups and napkins. As Serena turned away from the trash can, she saw him. Colonial Man. And he was heading straight for them.

Serena grabbed Carly's arm and pulled her towards the door of the museum.

"What are you doing?" Carly asked, shaking her arm free.

"It's him," Serena said, pushing Carly inside. "He must have been following us ever since the aquarium." She reached into her pocket and pulled out several bills and handed them to the cashier at the ticket counter. "This tour's on me," she said. "We'll give him the slip in here and go back to the subway, just like we did at the aquarium."

"Serena, this is crazy," protested Carly. "Let's just tell someone here."

"Tell them what?" asked Serena. "That a tour guide is after us because we took pictures of him giving artifacts to a janitor? They'll think we're crazy."

Not wanting to hear any more logical arguments, Serena ran up the steps to the second floor of the museum. Carly had no choice but to follow. As Serena looked down to the floor below, she saw Colonial Man buying his ticket. In another minute, he'd be up the steps.

They entered the nearest room, where troughs of water were ringed by children of all ages pushing boats under bridges, making waves, and splashing water everywhere. A large fountain spilled water over several ledges, and kids dropped dozens of colorful foam shapes in at the top and watched them tumble down.

Carly ran to a huge trough of water in the back of the room and ducked behind it. Serena spied a play station with a large space under it. She crawled under the table and quickly discovered why the space existed. A clear plastic dome rose over her head, jutting into the water trough above.

Serena stuck her head up into the bubble and was blasted from both ends with streams of water from kids operating water squirters. Through the plastic dome, Serena saw Colonial Man scanning the room for them. She hoped the water splashing down the bubble distorted her face enough that he wouldn't recognize her.

When Serena saw him march out of the room, she heaved a sigh of relief. Then she felt someone next to her and saw a boy waiting for her to get her head out of the bubble so he could have a turn. She crawled from under the table and hurried towards the water table Carly was behind. "He left the room," she whispered as she joined Carly.

"So let's make a run for it now while he's searching the next room."

"That was exactly my plan," said Serena.

They slowly stood up, surveying the room. They didn't see Colonial Man anywhere, so they raced through the crowd of noisy kids into the hallway and towards the steps. Serena grabbed the railing, preparing to pull herself around the corner and start down. Suddenly she stopped. Colonial Man stood midway down the flight of steps, waiting for them. Serena turned and bumped into Carly, who had just reached the top step, knocking her down.

"He's on the steps," said Serena, as she helped Carly up. They turned and began thundering up to the third floor. Serena looked over the railing and saw him round the corner below, still in pursuit. They reached the third floor and continued up the next flight of stairs, and then they ran out of steps and floors.

"Now where?" asked Carly.

Serena looked around and then headed to the right and into a room set up as a backyard ready for a sleepover. In the middle of the room sat a tent. "In there," said Serena. She opened up the tent flap, and the girls crawled in.

They spent the next several minutes catching their breath, wiping the sweat from their faces, and waiting for their heartbeats to slow down.

"Where do you think he is?" asked Carly, her voice choked with tears.

Serena moved closer to her and attempted to calm her fears. "I'm sure we gave him the slip," she said. "If we can get to the elevator, we can go right down to the first floor and then straight out the door."

"Where was the elevator?" asked Carly.

"I don't remember exactly," said Serena, "but I remember seeing a sign for one somewhere."

"Oh, I wish I'd had a chance to grab a map of the museum when we bought our tickets," said Carly. "Then I could see where everything is and find our way out."

"Forget the map," said Serena, "and get ready to go."

They waited for a large group of kids to congregate in the room before easing out from behind the tent flap. With Colonial Man nowhere in sight, the girls worked their way slowly out of the backyard room and back down the hall. They spied the sign on the wall directing them towards the elevator and picked up their pace. They rounded the corner, and, as the elevator came into view, so did Colonial Man. He was standing right in front of the door, blocking their escape route yet again.

CHAPTER SIXTEEN

A Narrow Escape

 When Colonial Man saw the girls, he strode towards them. Carly froze in her tracks, and Serena had to push her back towards the steps. She and Carly stomped down the stairs to the third floor. Just before they started down the next flight, Serena grabbed Carly's hand.

"Come on," she said. "I have an idea."

They hurried past the Construction Zone building area and a set of grandparents laughing as loudly as their young grandchildren. When they reached the Climbing Sculpture in the middle of the floor, Serena crept inside. Carly followed at her heels.

"I realized when we passed by on our way in that this sculpture is two stories tall," said Serena. "If we keep climbing, we'll end up on the second floor, and Colonial Man will still be looking for us on the third."

They crawled through pipes and into cages. A web of ropes appeared, and the girls swung and bounced from hole to hole, feeling like spiders crawling across a web. More tubes and tunnels followed, some with holes in them so they could look out. Serena peeked out and saw lots of people but none in costume.

Finally, they reached the second floor and climbed out of the sculpture. They hurried to the steps, thundered like elephants down to the first floor and charged out the front door. They looked behind them, but he wasn't following. As they passed the milk bottle and started toward the bridge, they exhaled loudly, sure they'd ditched him this time.

Serena took a final look back at the museum and stopped dead in her tracks.

Inside the glass-enclosed elevator, which ran on the outside of the building to provide a view of the city to its occupants, was a figure that, even from this distance, Serena could tell had on colonial clothes.

"Unbelievable," she said.

"What?" questioned Carly.

Serena pointed to the elevator.

"Well, I believe it," said Carly, angrily. "We didn't lose him at all."

"He probably figures we're going back for the pictures and then will confront us, demanding we give them to him."

"He's wrong there," said Carly. "Because we aren't going back for the pictures. We're going straight back to the Common and wait for the bus to come."

"But we've come this far," said Serena, starting in on her arguments to get Carly to agree to go back for them. "We can't quit now."

"Serena, we're in danger. I'm scared, and you should be, too. Let's just notify the police back at the Common and let them handle it. If they're interested in our pictures, we can always pick them up tomorrow."

"But the man will be gone by then. He'll know we contacted police, and he'll warn the others in the smuggling ring. His buddies won't show up for work, the artifacts will disappear and so will Colonial Man. Even if we do get the pictures tomorrow, by the time we get them to the authorities, everyone and everything will be long gone."

"Well, I just don't care anymore," argued Carly loudly. "I'm done with trying to save artifacts that I don't care about one bit."

Serena was ready to reply, but then she stopped. Carly's voice had an edge to it she'd never heard before. They'd argued plenty of times, and Carly could get really mad at her insistence to do something she didn't want to. But this time she heard fear underneath the anger and decided to push no further.

They reached South Station and the Red Line and waited for the train. Colonial Man showed up a few minutes later. He stood over by the wall, watching the girls. When the headlights of the train made their first faint appearance in the tunnel, the usual pandemonium struck as folks rushed towards the edge of the platform. Serena and Carly, caught up in swell of people, were pushed through the doors and onto the train.

Serena grabbed an empty seat, but once the train began

moving, she stood up and gave the seat to Carly. She held onto the handrail along the seat and prepared to make her move. As the train slowed during its approach to Downtown Crossing, Serena leaned over to Carly.

"Carly, I have to do this. Please understand. I respect your decision not to come with me, but I have to get the pictures."

The doors slid open, and Serena leaped off along with several others. Before Carly could even react, the doors had closed. Serena looked through the window and saw Carly, her eyes bugged out and her mouth forming Serena's name. Serena sighed, hoping Carly could forgive her for abandoning her. But with a little luck, she could get the pictures and meet up with her back at the Common.

After riding the T back to State Street, Serena followed the tunnel back to the entrance and hiked the steps to the street. She knew Colonial Man had to be back there somewhere but didn't want to look. She just hoped he did nothing more than follow her until she could alert the chaperones when the bus arrived.

But where was the photo shop? Where was the Old South Meeting House? Serena looked one way and then the other, trying to figure out where she was. It suddenly dawned on her that she was standing right in front of the Old State House. But how did she get there? The Old South Meeting House came before the Old State House on the Freedom Trail. When they'd gotten off at State Street before, they had been right near the Old

South Meeting House. Serena's only conclusion was that there must have been an exit closer to the Old South Meeting House that she should have taken.

She tried to calmly determine in which direction the meetinghouse was. But she only become more anxious as the sights and sounds of people, cars, buses, and sirens whirled around her, crowding her head so she couldn't think. Her heart began pounding and she felt lightheaded. She bent over a bit, attempting to alleviate the dizziness, and saw the brick path near her feet that would lead her back to her destination a few blocks away.

"Are the pictures for Serena Marlowe done yet?" she asked the clerk after arriving at the photo store.

"Let's see," said the clerk. She began hunting through a bin labeled M. "Nope, I'm afraid not."

"But it's been over two hours since I dropped them off!" cried Serena.

The girl searched through a stack of envelopes containing film waiting to be put through the developing machine. "Oh, they're being processed right now."

Serena sighed with relief. When they were finished, she opened the envelope and pulled out the photographs. Carly had done it. She'd gotten good, clear pictures of Colonial Man and Colonial Woman together. She had shots of his checking out the artifacts at the Old State House. The pictures inside the *Constitution*'s gift shop were a little dark, but you could still make out the two men and the envelope passed between them. The photos taken at the aquarium also showed an envelope as well as the artifacts being dropped into the janitor's trash bag.

Then Serena studied the photos Carly had taken of Colonial Man and the man who'd met him in Quincy Market for lunch. She knew the man looked familiar. Carly had gotten a portion of his face from the side when she moved in for the shot. But she had been far enough away that the face was still small and the features hard to distinguish.

At that moment, Serena looked up and saw a self-serve photographic copier and enlarger machine against the back wall with which she could produce a new set of prints exactly like the originals, or even bigger. She scanned the directions on it and placed the shots of the thief and his lunch buddy in the machine. After focusing in on the second man's face, Serena hit the enlarging button until it grew several sizes larger. "Bingo!" she said out loud. She pushed a button to make the print.

As she studied the enlarged photo, she knew she was right. Although she couldn't remember his name, this was the assistant city treasurer she'd seen on the news the first night of camp, who'd been arrested for changing the account books and pocketing city money. Serena guessed he'd been released until he went to trial.

"There has to be a connection between his stealing of city funds and the moving of artifacts out of the city," muttered Serena to herself. "Maybe he's the mastermind of the whole operation."

As she placed the print with the enlarged head into the envelope, Serena looked out the window. She still didn't see him anywhere, but she knew Colonial Man was out there, close by, waiting for her to leave with the pictures. She was sure he would approach her and demand she turn over the pictures and the negatives. What would he do if she didn't give them to him? Then, as if someone had turned on a light in her brain, an idea began to light up inside her.

She turned back to the copier, stuck in the entire set of pictures, and hit the copy button. She knew that if she turned over the packet of pictures to Colonial Man, the first thing he'd do would be to make sure the negatives were there, too. But hopefully he didn't know about photographic copiers and that there was one in the store. When she gave him the photo envelope, he would leave her alone, never suspecting she had a second set hidden in the back of her shorts.

After paying for the photos, Serena carefully placed the packet of duplicates beneath the elastic in her shorts and pulled her shirt over it. As she walked out of the store, boldly swinging the original set of prints at her side, she glanced across the street and saw Colonial Man near the same place she'd caught a glimpse of him when she and Carly had left the shop earlier in the day.

Serena looked up the street and saw a T sign, and realized that this was where she should have gotten off the T in the first place. As she began walking toward it, she glanced back, jumped slightly, and then walked faster, all to let Colonial Man know that she'd seen him and was scared, or at least pretending to be.

Up ahead she saw a bench and slowed down. After sneaking a peek behind her to make sure he was watching, she placed the bag on the bench. She continued on towards the subway, but slowly, waiting to take a final look at Colonial Man. He should be heading the other way, now that he had the evidence linking him to the stolen artifacts.

But when she turned her head, she froze, stunned to see him still in pursuit, the pictures gripped in his hand. Why hadn't her plan worked? He had both the pictures and the negatives. How did he suspect she had another set of prints?

She reached around and felt the pictures in her shorts only to discover the packet had wriggled up her back several inches with the movement of her body as she walked. The outline of the thick envelope had to be clearly visible beneath her shirt. Fearing it would work completely loose and fall out, she grabbed the packet and gripped it tightly in her hand.

Now she was getting scared, for real. Colonial Man had no intentions of dropping his pursuit until he had the second set of pictures. She knew he would make his move soon, probably when there was a crowd of people around so no one would notice when he snatched them from her hand. All she wanted to do now was make it back to the Common, find Carly and explain everything to the chaperones, who could alert the police.

But which train went to Boston Common? As she entered the Downtown Crossing station, she tried to remember the name of the station near the Common. She studied the diagram of the Orange and Red Lines that was on the wall. She heard a train coming and knew she had to decide fast. She saw her pursuer come onto the platform and, in a panic, lined up to get on the Orange Line train slowing in front of her, hoping it would go towards the Common. As the door closed, she fell into a seat, her pulse racing and her hands clammy. She gathered her bearings and looked at the line diagram on the wall of the car showing all the stops to the train's final destination. The next stop was Chinatown.

"Chinatown?" Serena muttered. "Is this the right train?"

CHAPTER SEVENTEEN

Panic on the Common

 Serena read the names of the other stops listed for the outbound Orange Line: New England Medical Center, Back Bay, Massachusetts Avenue, Ruggles, Roxbury Crossing, and several more. None sounded familiar to Serena.

"Excuse me," said Serena to the woman beside her. "I'm trying to get to the Common."

"You're going the wrong way, honey," she said. "You need to go back to the Red Line and take it to Park Street."

She thanked the woman and rode in silence, not believing she'd made such a stupid mistake. If only Carly had been there.

Finally the train pulled alongside the lighted platform of the Chinatown stop. She got out and followed the signs to the platform on the other side of the tracks and waited for a train to take her in the opposite direction. A clock on the wall showed it was ten minutes to five. She was cutting it close on meeting the bus and hoped there would be no more snags in her travel.

When she arrived back at Downtown Crossing, she followed the signs for the Red Line and Park Street. She found a bench and sat down, suddenly tired and ready for her investigation to be over. After a moment she looked around her. And there he was, sitting against the wall and smiling at her, almost mocking her. Colonial Man knew she'd made a mistake and had simply been waiting for her to show up here again.

He got up and started moving towards her. Serena looked around for a police officer, a guard, somebody to help her. She stood up and slid towards the steps, prepared to make a quick getaway to the street. If only the train would come! In a few minutes she'd be back at the Common.

"Attention, please. Attention," blasted a voice from the speakers on the wall. "A train has experienced mechanical problems between Downtown Crossing and Park Street, temporarily closing that portion of the line. Please exit to the street and board the city buses parked there. They will take you to the Park Street station where you can board the Red Line or connect to the Green Line. Your cooperation is appreciated."

"I don't believe this!" said Serena as she raced up the steps. Parked on the street were four city buses. She jostled along with other frustrated train-turned-bus riders who were eager to get to Park Street to make their next train connection. Serena was anxious to get on a bus, too, so she could avoid a confrontation with Colonial Man.

"Will this bus drop me off right at the Park Street station?" Serena asked the driver as she boarded the bus. She couldn't afford any more mistakes or delays.

"Yes, miss," he said. "Just have a seat. We'll be under way shortly."

The shortly became longer and longer. More people crowded onto the bus. Serena kept watching for Colonial Man to board. She didn't see him, but he most certainly had gotten on one of the other buses.

They sat and sat while the other buses filled up. Serena glanced at the watch on the wrist of the man sharing her seat. It said 5:10. The bus would already be at the Common! She hoped Carly could convince them to wait for her. But what if they didn't? Serena didn't even want to think about it.

Finally, the bus driver sat down and closed the door. He yanked the gearshift forward, and the bus inched away from the curb and into the busy city traffic. The other buses followed. Every so often, the bus driver jammed on the brakes and mumbled about a stupid driver who switched lanes suddenly and cut him off.

Serena fidgeted in her seat, wishing there were some way she could make the bus go faster. Finally she could just make out some greenery up ahead in the next block. Her mind raced as she prepared to exit the bus and look for Carly and the police. She hoped she could explain everything fast enough to the authorities so they could nab Colonial Man before he got away.

The bus pulled over and stopped right in front of the Park Street station. Serena was out of her seat and at the door before the driver even opened it. When he did, Serena bolted through the door like she'd been shot out of a cannon. She looked around for her camp bus but didn't see it anywhere. She ran to the path into the Common and searched the dwindling crowds for Carly but with no luck. Where was everybody? She was a little late, but they wouldn't leave without her! They couldn't!

Then she remembered that the guys had to be picked up at Fenway Park at 5:30. Maybe her group had had to leave to go get them and would come back. That was it, Serena was sure. She just had to keep hold of the pictures until they returned.

But there was Colonial Man, getting off the third bus. Serena continued walking briskly, turning her head every few seconds. He entered the Common and pursued her down the path. Serena looked again. He was gaining on her! She started trotting, weaving in and out among the people strolling on the path, envying their leisurely pace.

Her steps quickened until she was jogging, then running. Her feet pounded on the walkway as her heart pounded inside her chest. Sweat formed on her forehead, and her cheeks felt flushed. Her fingers, in a white-knuckled grip, dug into her skin through the layers of the paper bag. She was almost to the Frog Pond. She kept running, then turning, running then turning, pounding, heaving, sprinting, gasping!

"Halt!" shouted a voice. Serena slid to a stop on some loose gravel on the path and looked over her left shoulder. There stood a woman holding a gun aimed right behind Serena at Colonial Man. Several people in the area screamed. Everyone

scattered, frantic to escape the unfolding scene.

"Halt. Police," came a voice from the other side of the path.

"Give it up," said another. "You're surrounded."

Serena turned around to see a woman and two men with their weapons aimed right at Colonial Man, who had stopped just a few feet behind her. Another man and a woman charged up the hill from the Frog Pond off to her left. She heard a police siren and saw flashing lights.

Bewildered, Serena, cemented in her tracks, stared as two of the plainclothes police grabbed Colonial Man, wrestled him to the ground and handcuffed him behind his back. The other cops holstered their guns and gathered around Serena.

"Are you Serena Marlowe?" asked one of the women.

All Serena could do was nod.

One of the other men switched on his two-way radio. "She's okay," he said. "And we have the suspect in custody."

Serena heard a faint cheer coming from behind the pavilion down on the embankment along the edge of the Frog Pond. Within a few seconds, she saw familiar figures racing up the hill towards her.

As Serena's brain began functioning again, she realized who it was. "Carly!" she yelled, and started running across the grass.

"Serena!" shouted Carly.

They met midway between the path and the pond and locked in an enormous bear hug. Beth and Haley appeared then, and began hugging her as well. The two chaperones and the rest of

the girls from the bus gathered around Serena, and the entire group escorted her back up to the path to the officers and the gathering crowd.

Two of the undercover cops joined them while the other three held onto Colonial Man. Several uniformed police had arrived to keep back the crowds.

"I'm Detective Blackwell," said the woman. "And this is my partner, Detective Putnam."

"You are one lucky young lady to have such a persistent friend," said Detective Putnam, as he looked at Carly.

"She approached a uniformed patrolman and began telling him some crazy story about stolen artifacts, pictures, and a man dressed in a colonial costume who had been chasing the two of you," explained Detective Blackwell.

"He radioed the station and told Carly's tale. Several of the officers had investigated the reports of the missing duck and tea, but they couldn't figure out how the two of you got involved in the whole thing."

"But then the bus showed up with your friends here, and they said you'd gotten pictures of some stuff missing from the Paul Revere House," added Detective Blackwell.

"At any rate," said Detective Putnam, "since you hadn't shown up to meet your bus, we began to take Carly's story a little more seriously. Five of us detectives quickly hatched a plan to position ourselves on the Common as ordinary people. We raced down here a short time ago, prepared to wait until you showed up."

"I sure hoped you'd show up," said Carly. "I was so worried about you. I couldn't believe it when you dashed off the train like that. I knew the only way I could help you was to alert the police. But I had this fear that maybe you'd gotten lost and were riding the T the wrong way or that Colonial Man had hurt you or something."

"Carly, I'm not that bad with directions," said Serena, "and I planned all along to lead him back to the Common so he could be captured."

"Well, it was a pretty risky plan," Detective Blackwell said, chiding her gently.

"But we do need to get the full story from you," Detective Putnam said. "First we need to take your suspected thief into custody and find out who he is and question him."

"You go on back to the university, rest up a bit, and get something to eat. We'll be out later to get your story and see your pictures," added the other detective.

"Pictures!" exclaimed Serena, suddenly remembering the last place Carly had taken pictures. "Inside the aquarium we saw Colonial Man pass off the stolen papers and book to a janitor. After he gave the man an envelope—I'm sure it was full of money—the janitor put the artifacts into the bag he was using to collect the trash. You have to notify the people there and check the trash before this guy leaves with it or gives it to somebody else."

The two detectives stared at each other, unsure what to make of this newest part of the story. Detective Putnam switched on his radio and called into headquarters. Within minutes, two officers had been dispatched to the aquarium to check out Serena's tale.

As more uniformed officers gathered at the scene, the crowd began to disperse, and two patrolmen began to lead Colonial Man towards a police cruiser parked near the entrance of the Common.

"We'll see you a little later, then," said Detective Putnam to Serena.

As Colonial Man was ushered past them, he scowled angrily at Serena.

"If what you say is true about him, Serena," said Detective Blackwell, "you saved Boston from losing part of its historical heritage."

"Oh, it's true, all right," she assured the officers. She held up her bag with the pictures in it right at Colonial Man's face. "I've got proof."

CHAPTER EIGHTEEN

Boston's History Preserved

On their return to Boston University, all the girls dropped their belongings off in their rooms and then headed to the dining hall. When Serena appeared, everyone stood up and cheered. Jon and Derek and the rest of the boys had been picked up at the ballpark by another bus after the chaperones had alerted the hockey camp administrators of the situation at the Common. They waved Serena, Carly, Beth, and Haley over to the seats they'd saved for them.

"Our artifact saver," said Derek as Serena approached. "Allow me to pull out Detective Serena's chair."

Serena giggled as she sat down.

"We are most impressed," said Jon, giving her a round of applause.

"Yeah," said Derek. "Even my dad would be impressed with your crime solving skills."

"The details, the details," said Jon anxiously.

"I just relayed half the story to the girls on the bus," said Serena.

"So start again," Derek said. "We want to hear everything."

Serena, and occasionally Carly, retold the story of chasing the colonial man, taking pictures to provide proof, and then how he chased them. She finished the story as they finished their dessert. Just as Serena was washing her chocolate cake down with some milk, the dining hall became quiet. Everyone turned towards the door and saw a man and woman walking towards Serena.

"Oh, it's Detectives Blackwell and Putnam," said Serena.

"Hello, Serena," said Detective Blackwell. "I hope we've given you enough time to eat and rest a bit."

"Refueled and ready to go," she answered, wiping chocolate crumbs from her mouth with her napkin.

"Could we speak with you in your dorm's lounge?" asked Detective Putnam.

"And we need to see your pictures," added Detective Blackwell.

"Sure," Serena said. She looked at her friends around the table. "Would it be okay if my friends joined us?"

"Yeah, I guess that won't be a problem," Detective Blackwell answered.

The group walked over to the lounge in Sleeper Hall and settled themselves in couches and chairs. Serena returned to her room to gather her copies of Carly's pictures.

"First of all, we have good news," began Detective Blackwell after Serena had rejoined them. "The officers sent to the aquarium found the trash bag with the artifacts in one of the janitor's trucks. He's been arrested and is being questioned as we speak."

"What about Colonial Man?" asked Serena.

"Well, we know who he is," said Detective Putnam.

"His name is Nathan Conner, and he's a respected businessman in the community," explained Detective Blackwell. "But here's the crazy part. He's also on the board of directors of the Boston Historical Preservation Association."

Beth and Haley inhaled sharply. Jon whistled.

"Unbelievable!" exclaimed Serena. "One of the very people who's supposed to protect artifacts is stealing them."

"So what are you charging him with?" asked Derek.

"Nothing yet," said Detective Putnam. "He called his lawyer, and he's refusing to speak with us. We didn't find any artifacts in his backpack, so we don't have any evidence of his involvement with stealing them. The only unusual thing in his possession is a small ring that's stuck on his pinky finger, but wearing jewelry isn't a crime."

"What did you find in his backpack?" asked Carly.

"We found two envelopes containing a large amount of money, over twenty thousand dollars in all. We also found a notebook with diagrams and drawings in it. There was also a paper with a lot of names listed on it along with what looks like a grocery list."

"But having that stuff isn't illegal," said Derek. "You need solid proof of his connection to the artifacts to make a case."

"You're right," said Detective Putnam. He turned to Serena. "We need to see your pictures, and we need you to tell us exactly

what artifacts were stolen and where you last saw them."

"Didn't Colonial Man have the other pack of pictures with him at the Common?" asked Serena.

The detectives gave her a puzzled look. "Other pictures?" questioned Detective Blackwell.

Serena explained her ploy of copying the first set and then leaving them for him to pick up, hoping he wouldn't realize she still had a set with her.

"Well, we didn't find any," answered Detective Blackwell. "But since we thought the only pictures were yours, we didn't look for the set he had. He probably dropped them when we all descended on him to get rid of any evidence connecting him with the crime."

Serena nodded and began telling her story for a third time, showing them Carly's pictures at each place where Colonial Man was stealing artifacts, planning to steal them, or selling them to someone. She explained that the drawings were diagrams of the rooms and display cases in the Old State House.

"Colonial Man collected the duck from Colonial Woman at Paul Revere's house," Serena continued. "He left it with the clerk in the gift shop at the *Constitution* Museum, who gave him an envelope in exchange."

"We're sure that he stole a foot warmer from the Old North Church," added Carly, "but I wasn't able to get a picture of his doing it."

"Oh, so you're our photographer?" asked Detective Putnam.

Serena frowned. "I thought I'd mentioned that," she mumbled.

"Well, your pictures are sure going to provide us with the proof we need to make a case against this man," said Detective Putnam, shaking his head in amazement as he looked at each print.

"What did he do with the foot warmer?" Detective Blackwell asked.

Serena offered her speculation that he'd passed it off to someone who met him in the Bunker Hill tower. "I also saw the TV report about tea missing from the Old North Church Museum. I'm sure there's a connection."

"We'll check it out."

"Oh!" exclaimed Serena. "Speaking of connections . . . " She hunted through the pictures until she found the one with the enlarged face. "Look familiar?"

The two detectives stared at each other. "I don't believe it," said Detective Putnam.

"Assistant City Treasurer McElwee is involved in this?" asked Detective Blackwell.

"I think he might be the ringleader of the whole operation," said Serena.

The two detectives stood, preparing to return to the station to present the incriminating pictures to Mr. Conner. All at once, Serena jumped up, too. "I almost forgot another stolen artifact," she said. "The candle mold from Paul Revere's house."

"Candle mold?" asked Detective Putnam.

"That's what started Serena on this whole smuggling thing," said Carly. "She took Polaroid pictures in Paul Revere's house and was convinced that one picture shows the mold on the floor and the next picture doesn't."

"We all thought her imagination had run amok," said Beth.

"But when we returned to Paul Revere's house today," continued Serena, "the mold was right where it had been. I'm no antiques specialist, but I doubt this mold was authentic. I think if you check it out, you'll find out that the current candle mold is a cheap imitation."

"Well, we're sure glad you knew that artifacts can be valuable, and possessed enough caring and determination to save these city treasures, Serena," said Detective Blackwell.

"And we're equally appreciative of your photographic skills, Carly," said Detective Putnam, "and your quick involvement of the police. The city of Boston is indebted to you both."

The pair of officers left then, but said they'd return later that evening for Serena's written statement of the day's events and to return her pictures, once they'd made their own copies to keep as evidence.

Serena and Carly and their group of friends lingered in the lounge, deciding to stay there until the detectives came back. They would all be heading home the next day, so they wanted to spend as much time together as possible. While they waited,